SO-AIH-146

THE
LONG
CRY

Mildred Offerle

CONCORDIA PUBLISHING HOUSE
SAINT LOUIS, MISSOURI

Concordia Publishing House, Saint Louis 18, Missouri
Concordia Publishing House, Ltd., London, W. C. 1
Copyright 1960 by Concordia Publishing House

Library of Congress Catalog Card No. 60-13114

Manufactured in the United States of America

$\mathcal{M}$IRIAM, daughter of Simeon, lifted the long skirt of her robe and raced across the courtyard of her Judean home and out the gateway onto the road, where a caravan was approaching. Then she stopped and flushed in embarrassment. The caravan which she had heard was not that of Anak, her father's trusted servant. Rather, it was Nebuzaradan's, the tall captain of the Babylonian hordes. Seeing Miriam, he halted and walked toward her.

"How you do grow!" Nebuzaradan laid a friendly hand on her shoulder. He spoke solemnly, but there was laughter in his eyes. "I thank you for the eagerness of your welcome, but I fear it was thoughts of another that set the wings to your feet. You will find him resting beneath the sycamore tree."

Miriam's glance darted quickly past him, wondering how he could know. But it was only Urusar who sat there, smiling his lazy, teasing smile.

"It is not good that my friend, the mighty Nebuzaradan, be left standing outside the gate," she said quickly. "Come, we will go inside, and Deborah will bring you a cool drink."

Nebuzaradan smiled down at her. "Truly, I find it a charming offer. But see, already your father comes."

Miriam watched and wondered as her father greeted the Babylonian with cool politeness. Simeon was an Israelite, of the tribe of Judah, and a proud man. He patiently endured the yoke of Babylon, judging it to be Jehovah's will, but he had no love for the man whose hand had laid that yoke upon him.

As the two men walked off together, Miriam turned and slowly approached Urusar, who was waiting for her. He looked up at her lazily. "It is kind of you to bless me with your company," he teased.

Miriam tilted her head a little to look down at him from the corner of her eye. Then she let her glance sweep on to where a dozen armed guards refreshed themselves and their horses at the well.

"You have come all the way from Jerusalem," she mused thoughtfully, "just so that your uncle might speak with my father?"

Urusar nodded and smiled.

"It must be very important business, for it is a far distance to travel." She looked down, hoping that he would explain their business.

"Yes," he agreed, in a tantalizing way, "and the day is hot."

She looked back to where the armed guards stood waiting. "It amuses Urusar to think that I can scarcely bear my curiosity," she thought, "but I shan't give him the satis-

2

faction of asking." Aloud she said, "When I heard you at the gate, it was another I expected."

"And you are disappointed?"

She lifted her chin and tensed her lips to suppress a smile. "A little."

"Ah, I wondered why we received so eager a welcome. It was for another." He looked up and sighed deeply in pretended sadness. "And this other, is he as handsome as I?"

Miriam laughed in spite of herself. For some reason Urusar could always make her laugh. "You are a vain person, Urusar. This day Anak returns from many months of traveling on business for my father."

"I have seen Anak." Urusar frowned thoughtfully. "Is it vanity for me to say that I am by far the more handsome?"

"It is true that Anak's beauty is all in his goodness," Miriam agreed, "but it is not only for Anak that I wait. A messenger came last night to tell us that Asahel is traveling with him from Jerusalem. It has been many months since last I saw Asahel, but, as I remember him, he had grown quite tall and easy to look upon."

"And you prefer this stranger to me?" Urusar challenged playfully.

Miriam was thoughtful for a moment. She knew he was teasing her. Yet he spoke correctly when he called Asahel a stranger. How could she be certain that she liked Asahel best, or that she would like him at all, now that he was becoming a man. "I am his betrothed," she said quietly.

Urusar got slowly to his feet and measured her with a long and knowing look. Then he laughed. "You are but a child!"

"When the season of reaping comes, I will have seen fourteen ingatherings of the grain," Miriam protested, looking haughtily up at him with every inch of her small stature.

3

"For twelve years," she added, "I have been betrothed to Asahel. It was his mother's dying wish."

"Betrothed when a babe! I have heard of such." He looked at her in wonder, then shrugged and changed the subject. "Already the shadows are lengthening. I have foolishly been sitting when I should have been easing the cramps from my legs. Come, walk with me. We will walk toward Jerusalem; perhaps we may meet your friends as they approach."

Miriam shook her head. "I would, but I may not. My mother says that it is no longer safe, now that our land swarms with enemy soldiers."

"Of course, and she is right," Urusar agreed. "But remember, my little friend, it is not the Babylonian soldiers alone whom you must fear. Watch carefully the deserting scum of your own armies."

"But they are our friends! Our own people!"

"I, too, am your friend, little Miriam."

Miriam looked up at the tall young man beside her. In his eyes she could read his loneliness, and she felt a sudden pity for him. "Yes," she said softly, "you are my friend." She took his hand and drew him slowly toward the house. "We will go into the courtyard. I would hear of your sister Abilath. Tell me, does she grow stronger?"

"When last we heard, she was still unable to leave her couch."

"I would hear more."

"Our talk must wait," Urusar said softly. "They would speak with you. I pray that my uncle's mission may be successful."

As Miriam looked up, she saw Deborah standing in the doorway and motioning her to hurry.

"Now mind your manners!" Deborah scolded nervously as she hurried Miriam across the courtyard.

4

Miriam glanced impatiently at her old nurse. Deborah was always scolding and forever reminding her to do the things that she had always done.

"Come," her father said, as she entered the room. "Come, sit beside me." He put his arm around her shoulders and smiled down at her, but she sensed a sadness in his smile. "We are faced with making an important decision, my daughter. Today your good friend Nebuzaradan has stopped with an invitation from his niece, the lady Abilath, that you pay her a visit."

"You mean that I am to go to Babylon, as so many others of our people have gone?" Miriam asked in surprise.

Nebuzaradan smiled. "No, Miriam, you will not go as a slave but as a friend and guest in my house."

"Oh, Father! That is wonderful news! I have heard so much about the lady Abilath, and now I will have the chance to know her — if you desire it."

Miriam looked eagerly at her mother, who responded with a sad smile.

"I assure you, my good Simeon, it is for her own protection that I urge you to let her go," Nebuzaradan insisted.

Simeon drew himself up proudly. "What happens to each of us is in the hands of Jehovah. The child will go to Babylon because the visit pleases her and not to escape the coming punishment of my people. Whether she stays, or whether she goes, she is a daughter of Judah."

It all seemed like a strange dream to Miriam. The thought of visiting Abilath excited her. She should have been completely happy, but she was not. How could she be, when neither her mother nor her father were? She turned to Nebuzaradan and asked, "Will you go with me?"

"No," he replied, "you will travel with an official of the king, a man named Samgar-nebo.

"Will Mother go with me?"

"Ah, my daughter," Simeon sighed deeply, shaking his head. "I wish that it might be so."

"I am sorely needed here," her mother said slowly. A worried frown wrinkled her forehead. "How can we let her go without either Deborah or me? And Deborah is too old for such a journey."

"If she goes, then Leah, the daughter of Jogli, shall go with her," Simeon decided.

"Have no fear for her safety, my friends," Nebuzaradan assured them. "Samgar-nebo will let no harm befall her. It may also please you to know that my niece has a fine nurse who will care for her also, a Judean woman called Hannah. You can trust her, for she will care for your daughter as for her own."

Simeon sat fingering his full neat beard. "I wish that there were more time in which to consider," he said thoughtfully. "It is not that I doubt the wisdom of your words, Nebuzaradan, but only . . ."

"I understand," Nebuzaradan interrupted. "Let me say that I will place a litter in the caravan of Samgar-nebo for the lady Miriam and her servant. When the caravan arrives, on the third day, you will have made your decision."

"You speak wisely," Simeon answered, bowing low.

Nebuzaradan bowed low in return, and laid a friendly hand on Miriam's arm. "The gods willing, when next we meet, it will be in my own house in Babylon."

Miriam nodded. Her lips were strangely stiff when she tried to smile. She could understand that her parents might be unhappy at the thought of being separated from her, but what was the meaning of this talk of danger? She frowned, then shrugged and smiled.

"I am going to see Abilath," she whispered to herself, forgetting everything else. "I am going to Babylon." And, for the first time, she believed it.

6

She hurried down the hall. Her news was too good to keep — she must tell Leah at once. Nebuzaradan and his men were mounting their horses as she slipped from the house and hurried down the path to the abode of Jogli, chief of her father's shepherds. She found Leah kneeling in the shade, pounding meal.

"I came as soon as I could," she panted. "I have good news for you."

Leah looked up, startled. One of her heavy black braids slipped over her shoulder and dipped into the meal. But as she nodded eagerly, it flipped out again unnoticed. "I have heard," she said.

"You know? But how could you?"

"Deborah has told us. She is even now inside talking with my mother."

"Oh, Leah!" Miriam exclaimed, throwing her arms around her friend, "It will be such fun!"

"Yes," Leah agreed, "it will be fun, but there will be great changes in our lives."

"What do you mean?"

"For me there will be more responsibility because I will be serving you. Then, also . . ."

"You are thinking that we will now be lady and servant," Miriam interrupted. "Has it not always been so, Leah? Certainly you do not think that it will change my feelings of friendship toward you!"

"It is not only that. It is also that my mother feels I am too young for such responsibilities. I would like so much to go with you!"

"Why do you always go looking for things to fret about?" Miriam smiled down at her friend's thin shoulders, bending above the grinding stone. "Do not fear, my father will arrange everything."

Leah looked up and laughed. "It will be fun." She

7

attacked the meal with furious pounding. "Wait while I take this inside and we can walk back together. Deborah said that I must stay with you now, so that she may teach me the things which I must know."

As the two girls walked slowly back along the path, Leah stopped to pick a flower. She tucked it into Miriam's hair at the place where the braid began. "I will be dressing your hair with a golden band, and every day you will wear fine robes. You shall be the finest lady in all Babylon!" Leah exclaimed, bowing low.

"Stop teasing. If you do not, you will frighten me before we even get started!"

"I have heard that they have many festivals there and great festal dinners." To Leah it was an exhilarating prospect.

"So have I heard. Yet it is not likely that I shall get to attend any of them. I doubt that Lady Abilath is strong enough to attend many festivals. Anyway, it is not likely that an Israelite would eat at a Babylonian table." Miriam knew this was true, but she could not conceal the overtone of wishing in her voice.

Leah heard it and turned to smile at her. "You know that Nebuzaradan is a great man and that you are to be a guest in his house."

"But we must never forget that we are of Judah."

Leah sobered. "Yes, I see what you are thinking," she said. "It may well be that we will find we cannot eat the Babylonian foods, for they may be forbidden foods. But how are we to know?"

"Again you are worrying, Leah!" Miriam chided. "Remember, there is the nurse, Hannah, who will instruct us in such matters."

Leah kicked a pebble from the path and turned to look thoughtfully across the countryside. "Does it not seem un-

8

fair that we should be laughing and happily planning while all the rest of Israel is in mourning?"

"Mourning?" Mariam looked up, bewildered, "Why do they mourn?"

"Did you not know that Nebuzaradan stopped on his way to meet Nebuchadnezzar and all his horde? They even now come to lay siege to Jerusalem."

Miriam shook her head sadly. "No one told me," she said. But now she understood why there had been so little happiness in the faces of her parents.

As she turned to look across the hills toward Jerusalem, she saw a caravan approaching. "Look, Leah," she cried, forgetting everything else, "it is Anak! Anak has come, and Asahel is with him!"

TWO

It was two days since Nebuzaradan's visit. They were two busy days into which her mother and Deborah had tried to crowd weeks of work and preparation. Once while they were busy, Miriam slipped, unnoticed, from the room. She walked down the stairway and across the courtyard to where the men sat talking. She sat down beside her father and let her gaze shift from Asahel to Caleb, his father, and back to her own father.

Asahel looked no different than he had on the last visit home, but Miriam noticed that there was a difference. On his last visit he had been treated as a child, even as they treated her. Today her father turned to him as a man, listening to his words and accepting his opinions.

Simeon was saying, "We have heard rumors that Zedekiah, our puppet king, is not well."

"He is not," Asahel answered quietly. "But his sickness is not a sickness of the body but rather of the mind."

Caleb laughed and there was something in the sound that frightened Miriam. She was sorry that she had slipped away from the house and come here, but she listened as Caleb remarked, "No wonder that Nebuchadnezzar no longer trusts the man he set on Israel's throne."

"Aye," her father agreed. "There were those who wondered from the start why Nebuchadnezzar chose him."

Asahel studied the strap of his sandal thoughtfully. "There are those who feel that Jerusalem might still be saved if Zedekiah would but listen to the counsel of Jeremiah, the prophet of Jehovah, rather than to the plottings of evil princes."

Simeon stroked his beard and nodded in agreement. "It is what we have believed all along, but you forget, my young friend, that throughout Israel there are many who say that Jeremiah is a traitor — both to Israel and to Jehovah."

"But do you not also agree that it seems strange that Jehovah should decree that all His people again go into exile? It is for saying this that they call him traitor. Why must we, the people of the Most High, become slaves of Babylon?" Asahel demanded heatedly.

"Silence!" Caleb demanded. "Would you question Jehovah, my son?"

Miriam shifted uneasily. Breaking into the silence that followed, she announced. "I am going to Babylon."

Caleb nodded. "It is good," he said. But she knew that he had not heard.

"It makes me very happy," she added, wishing that they were more interested. "Nebuzaradan himself stopped by to invite me."

10

"Nebuzaradan? Here?" Asahel asked in surprise. "What business had the Babylonian captain with the house of Simeon?" He looked at his father, and Miriam saw a quick signal of fear and suspicion pass between them.

"I just told you!" Miriam cried in exasperation. "No one ever listens to what I say!"

"Hush, Miriam!" her father ordered. He had seen the look too. "It has been no secret to either of you that Nebuzaradan stops at the well, or that he has shown friendship to my daughter," he answered angrily, but when he went on, he spoke more quietly, "I have been but waiting the proper time before telling you of these things. I see now that I should have told you before — for your interest in my daughter is nearly as great as my own. Nebuzaradan has within his household a beloved niece about Miriam's age, a girl named Abilath. She is a cripple. He but asks that Miriam visit the child for a time."

"This is the reason he gave?" Caleb demanded. "Does it not seem a strange request?"

Simeon tugged angrily at his beard before answering. "Nay, there is more. He thought it best that she not remain here in Judea. He also is fond of my daughter and fears for her safety. She shall go, but she is to stay only as long as we deem it necessary. Is it not better that she go as a guest? If I refuse, he may seize her and take her as a captive."

Asahel and Caleb nodded soberly. Caleb bowed low, "Forgive us, my friend, but these are trying times when a man is overly quick to suspect what he does not understand."

Simeon was about to reply, but, turning to Miriam, he said rather brusquely, "Leah would speak with you."

"Deborah wishes us to climb to the clearing where the herbs grow and gather them," said Leah as she handed a basket to Miriam and held one out for Asahel.

11

Asahel looked up at her in surprise. "That is women's work," he said somewhat defiantly.

"Would you let them wander through the hills unprotected?" Caleb demanded.

"Aye, Asahel," Simeon agreed, "it is better that you go. Deborah will not let the girls go wandering through the hills alone. Also, there are things which I would discuss, privately, with your father."

Asahel shrugged and took the basket, but Miriam knew that he was not happy about it. She looked up shyly and said, "It is kind of you to go with us. It has been weeks since either of us has been out of sight of the house."

Asahel looked down at her and grinned. "Do you think that I should carry a weapon, so that I can protect you properly?" he teased.

"The knife in your girdle will be sufficient," she answered.

The path to the clearing was steep, with many rocks to scramble over, or walk around. They raced and played at hide-and-seek along the way. Slowly the strangeness that Miriam had felt toward Asahel melted away. They were friends again, just as they had always been.

As they gathered the plants, they talked and laughed. Then, as Leah packed them into two of the baskets, Miriam picked up the third and examined it. Deborah had filled it with loaves and cheese and fruit for their lunch.

When Leah had finished, the three of them set off, climbing higher in search of a place in which to rest and eat.

"Let us stop here," Leah suggested when they came to a place where the path skirted the foot of a steep cliff.

"Look," Asahel called, "here is a large flat stone on which we can sit."

"It looks as though someone had set it here just for us," Miriam agreed happily.

12

Leah folded back the napkin that covered the basket. "If you will both be seated, I will serve you," she announced.

"We will all sit down," said Miriam. "There is no need for you to serve us."

"I believe that Leah is right, Miriam." Asahel sat down beside her. "Things are going to be quite different for both of you. I think that it is best if you begin this new relationship right away, so that neither of you will forget at some later time. It might have been better for both of you if you had not always been permitted to be together."

"How could it be better if we were not friends?" Miriam demanded. "You talk foolishness."

Asahel broke a large chunk from the loaf before he replied. "How can I explain if you refuse to understand?" And then, more good-naturedly, he added, "Then again, maybe you are right. It will mean that I can expect Leah to keep a sharp eye on you." He turned and grinned at Leah. "I think I can trust Leah to see that you behave."

"You can trust me," Leah replied, laughing.

Miriam nibbled thoughtfully at the crust of her bread, trying to decide whether or not they were laughing at her. Gazing casually around her, she noted a bush that seemed to grow out from the very rock at the edge of the cliff. It grew at a strange angle. She studied it for a time, then walked over to examine it. With an inviting smile she beckoned Asahel to join her.

They stepped around the bush and discovered a huge slab of stone that stood out a bit from the rest and partially covered a narrow hidden opening that looked like an entrance to a shadowy cave. Pausing long enough to call to Leah, he cautiously followed Miriam through the opening into a cave that was several feet wide and high enough for a man to stand erect.

Asahel took Miriam's hand and slowly they felt their

way through the darkness. Suddenly they noticed that the cave was a tunnel which led into a large, low-vaulted chamber. A faint light entered through the cracks in the fall of rock that formed its south wall. From the opposite wall they could see more tunnels running back into the hillside.

A movement at the far side of the chamber caused them both to stiffen. Out of the semidarkness came a man who slowly turned to face them. Asahel thrust Miriam behind him, and his hand reached for the knife in his girdle.

Miriam gasped in surprise when she saw her father's servant. "Anak! What are you doing here?"

"It is, rather, you who must answer that question," Anak replied sternly.

"We were gathering greens for Deborah."

Anak watched her closely as she spoke, and Miriam knew that he was not pleased.

"Is this Simeon's secret cave?" Asahel asked.

Anak nodded.

In the dim light, Miriam could see that Anak was standing before the entrance to a cavern space that was filled with bales and goatskin bags. She looked up at Asahel and saw that he had noticed it too. He frowned thoughtfully and asked, "Does Simeon plan that his family shall live here through this siege, even as his father's did before him?"

"It is not for me to know my master's plans, and it will be best if you do not mention that you were here. Indeed, it would be best if you forgot what you have seen and where you saw it."

"But I will be in Jerusalem! One day it may be of greatest importance that I know," Asahel insisted.

Anak shook his head. "Nay, if it be important that you know the way, Simeon himself will tell you. Now go."

Leah was gone when they emerged from the cave. They

14

called her name many times but received no answer. "Perhaps she thought that we were playing a trick on her and had gone home, leaving her behind," Miriam suggested.

"I told her to wait. You heard me."

"I heard you," Miriam agreed, "but did she?"

Asahel shrugged. "She cannot have gotten far. We must hurry."

Miriam looked thoughtfully back to the cave before hurrying after him. "Do you think we will live there again, as they did before?" she asked.

"Yes, I think you will. It is better than facing the abuses of the soldiers of Babylon."

Miriam nodded, remembering that the house was close to the road the soldiers would use — and they already visited the well.

THREE

The sun had set and darkness lay cool and fragrant over the countryside. Miriam leaned back and looked up at the stars as she drew her fingers across the strings of her lyre, strumming dreamy music for Asahel, who sat nearby. It had been an exciting day.

She was unusually aware of everything around her. Things that she had scarcely noticed yesterday were suddenly important. Tonight they were hers; tomorrow she would be gone.

She knew, without turning, that her mother sat quietly in the shadows, looking toward Jerusalem. She would be worrying about the battles to come, or perhaps she was

15

making more plans for the morrow. Miriam frowned. It seemed her mother was always either worrying or planning.

Nor did she have to look up at Asahel to know that he was watching her closely, as though trying to read her thoughts.

It was a night like many other nights when they had sat on the roof in the evening, awaiting her father. Yet it was not like any other night that Miriam had ever known, for it was filled with the magic of her plans and dreams of far-off places. But her happiness was tinged with the sadness of the oppression that was spreading across the land of Judah.

She drew her fingers slowly, string by string, across the lyre. "Soon I will see Babylon," she said softly, "and I have never seen Jerusalem. Tell me of Jerusalem, Asahel."

"Jerusalem?" he asked sharply. "What care you for Jerusalem? Would you not rather hear about Babylon?" He sat silent for a time and then added, more kindly, "Now, with the coming of Nebuchadnezzar and his troops to destroy the city of David, what is there to tell?"

"Have you no faith, Asahel? Surely Jehovah will preserve His holy city!"

Asahel made no answer, and Miriam looked around at him, trying to see what he might be thinking, but the night was dark. She drew her fingers across the lyre in a mournful chord, then impatiently muted it with her hand.

"Please tell me of the temple and the market place and the palaces of the rich," she begged. "I have never been to a city, but I know that Jerusalem must be the most beautiful of them all!"

Asahel shook his head slowly. "Those who are well-traveled say it is not so. But to me it seems a place of great beauty. I like the bustle of it. When I am not busy with my studies, I often walk through the streets and watch the people. Usually I see traders of many lands, but these last days they have been fleeing the city as from a pestilence. I fear it may be a long time before they return."

"And you?" Miriam asked. "Will you go back?"

"Yes, I must soon return," Asahel replied.

"There will be great danger, once the siege begins! Why must you go back? My father said that it was a blessing that you have come home. Your father grows old and has need of you here."

"I have Zedekiah's orders to return, but I would have returned anyway. Judah has need of men to stand against Nebuchadnezzar's forces. Soon enough there will be nothing here for me — or for your father. The coming and going of Nebuchadnezzar and his armies and their plundering will make this stretch of countryside of little use in the raising of flocks and grain. As for the danger, it is my place to be beside my king!"

Miriam wondered whether he was as sure of his bravery as he seemed to be. She knew that she would not have been if she had been in his place. Aloud she said, "I think you will make a brave soldier. Maybe Zedekiah will even make you a captain of his army."

Asahel was about to reply when the sound of voices at the outer gate floated up to them. They tensed, listening. There were footfalls on the stairway. And then a voice. "Peace be unto the household of Simeon." There was no mistaking the voice.

As Miriam and Asahel scrambled to their feet, her mother answered, "The peace of Jehovah and this household be unto you, Jeremiah. Rest here while I get food to refresh you and the good Baruch."

"Thy mother is, indeed, a good and wise woman," Jeremiah remarked as her footsteps faded away down the stairway. "Remember always, my child, that a worthy woman

17

is the crown of her husband. I would add that she is also the flame at which the hearts of her family are warmed."

"Aye," Baruch agreed softly.

"And you, little daughter of Simeon, will you sing for us while we await your father?" the prophet suggested.

Miriam bent her head over her lyre. She drew her fingers slowly across the strings. Ordinarily her songs were bright and happy songs, but these chords were gray with sadness and suffering:

> *Give ear, O shepherd of Israel,*
> *Thou that leadest Joseph like a flock,*
> *Stir up Thy might,*
> *And come to save us.*
> *Turn to us again, O Jehovah, God of hosts;*
> *Cause Thy face to shine*
> *And we shall be saved.*

When the last tones had swelled and faded, like some long cry floating down through the ages, Jeremiah said softly, "A psalm of deliverance. Why chose you such a song, my child?"

"Because Judah is in need of deliverance, and quite soon. Jehovah has delivered His children before and I know He can do so again."

"Ah, my child, my child, I would that there were even one with thy faith in a high place."

"Then you carry bad news to Zedekiah?" Asahel asked.

Jeremiah nodded, but before he could speak, Simeon's voice sounded out of the darkness at the head of the stairs. "Greetings, O prophet of Jehovah. Our poor house is blessed this night."

"Aye, and I am thankful to have reached its haven."

"You have traveled far?" Miriam asked.

"I have reached my destination."

18

There was weariness in his voice, and Miriam reached out her hand to lay it comfortingly in his. "It is good that you stay here for a while," she said.

Asahel was filled with the rumors, the fears, and the hopes that were now so much a part of life in Jerusalem. He blurted out, "Then you go not to Jerusalem to talk with Zedekiah?"

Jeremiah took a deep breath and stiffened his shoulders. He looked toward Jerusalem for a long time, in silence. "No, it is not yet time for me to go to Jerusalem, but even now a messenger is carrying Jehovah's words to the king. If he would hear more, let him send for me."

"And is it for us to know this message?" Simeon asked quietly.

Jeremiah rose to his full height. As he faced them, the lights of the night were caught and reflected in his eyes. When he spoke, his voice was deep and frightening. "The sin of Judah is written with a pen of iron, and with the point of a diamond; it is graven upon the tablet of their heart and upon the horns of their altars. Thus saith Jehovah, the God of Israel, 'Go speak to Zedekiah, king of Judah, and tell him, thus saith Jehovah: Behold, I will give this city into the hands of the king of Babylon, and he shall burn it with fire; and thou shalt not escape from his hands.'"

Asahel's voice broke through the grim silence that followed. "Has Jehovah, then, deserted His people in their hour of need?"

"Nay, my son," Simeon answered gently. "Say, rather, that Judah has deserted her God and turned to the idols of the pagan, and this is her punishment."

"But what of those who have not turned from the ways of Jehovah?" Asahel demanded.

"Be still!" his father ordered. "Would you question the

ways of the Most High? Would you bring down His wrath upon us all?"

"Nay, do not rebuke him," the prophet gently admonished Caleb "for he does not question God's ways. It is just that he would understand them. I would that there were more who cared enough to ask." Jeremiah paused and shook his head sadly. "Judah will have need of young men of faith. As for Jehovah's people, they must go to Babylon as Jehovah has ordained. Let them not forget the God of their fathers, for only through Him will they receive their deliverance."

FOUR

"Today is the day! Today is the day!" The words sang in Miriam's mind even before she was fully awake. She opened her eyes slowly. Observing Leah, who was already busy with her tasks, she smiled, remembering that her mother had kept both Leah and herself busy filling chests and bundles. It would take a sizable caravan of her father's pack animals to carry her own possessions and the gifts to the household of Nebuzaradan. "One would think I was never to return," she said aloud.

At the sound of Miriam's voice, Leah looked around in surprise and smiled. "It will be a beautiful day to begin our journey," she said happily. Remembering Miriam's words, she added, "Have you heard any talk of when we return?"

"My father has not told me so, but I am certain that when the time of harvest is over, he will send his servant

20

Anak to bring us home again." She would not admit it to Leah, but she, too, had a strange feeling that perhaps this was not an ordinary visit.

Miriam suddenly felt very much alone. She was not as certain as she had been that she wanted to go. "I am glad that you are going with me, Leah," she said, wondering whether she was going to be so foolish as to become homesick before she even got started.

Leah nodded, but made no answer.

Deborah came puffing into the room. She looked at Miriam in surprise and exclaimed, "Up with you, you lazy child! With so much to do, do you lie abed? Already a messenger has come with word that the caravan will arrive at the place of meeting before high noon."

Miriam laughed excitedly. All of her worries were forgotten. She bounded out of bed and threw her arms about her nurse. "Deborah, I love you so much!" she cried, squeezing the plump old woman in a tight hug. "You are always so kind to me. I only hope the nurse Hannah will be half as kind and wise."

"Your flattery doesn't deceive me, young lady," Deborah said brusquely. But her words could not hide the pleasure that shone in her eyes, or her sorrow at the thought of their parting. Turning to Leah, she added quickly, "Come, from now on it is for you to help your lady prepare herself for the day. I wish to see whether you have learned your lesson well."

The next hours sped by, riding the wings of the wind. There were so many things Miriam wished to do, so many farewells that must be made. She had scarcely begun when her mother came for her. "Come," she said, "your father has words for you."

Miriam went quickly to the room where her father conducted his business or where, when not busy, he studied

21

and meditated. She entered and found Jeremiah pacing slowly across the far side of the room, but her father was not there. She turned to leave. Jeremiah raised his hand in a small salute and said, "Wait, daughter of Simeon. It is I who would speak with you. I would counsel you before you go."

Miriam stood quietly waiting as he crossed the room to where she stood. She dared not look up after he had blessed her. She felt a strange fear of him. His nearness to Jehovah and his knowledge of things to come set him apart from other men. "It is a long journey that you take," he said, "but it is one that all our countrymen must soon make. Fear not, for many of our people have already gone before you to the villages of Kifil and Tel-abib.

"When you reach the house of Nebuzaradan, have the woman Hannah take you to Kifil, beside the river Chebar. There seek out one called Ezekiel, a priest of the Most High. Tell him that Jeremiah sent you to him. He will instruct you, and if any evil befalls you, heed what he tells you."

Miriam bowed low and thanked him as she left to go to her mother. Thinking of bidding her farewell, she was losing some of her zest for the journey to Babylon. Her steps slowed as she made her way to her mother's room. There had been a certain joy in saying farewell to the others. With her mother it was different — her mother was a part of everything that made up her life. It was like taking leave of a part of herself. She paused outside the door, then knocked and entered.

"I have a gift for you, Miriam," her mother said as she held up a gold bracelet. "May it be a token to remind you always to be good and kind and, above all, to walk always in the ways of our people."

"I will not be gone long," Miriam sobbed, throwing her arms about her mother and hugging her close.

"Nay," her mother agreed, smiling down at her. "It will not be for long, and time has a way of passing quickly."

She held her daughter in one last embrace. "Go now. Your father is waiting."

So it was that in the ninth year of the reign of Zedekiah, king of Judah, on the first day of the tenth month — the month called Tammuz — that Miriam, the daughter of Simeon, began her journey to Babylon.

Miriam trembled with excitement as she and Asahel and Leah mounted their donkeys and took their places behind the armed guards. Simeon was somewhere among the guards, but Miriam did not know where. At a shout from Anak they moved slowly forward.

"Asahel, I wish that you were to ride all of the way with us!" Miriam pleaded as she turned her face to meet the full sweep of the spicy wind. "Perhaps you could ride for an extra day before returning to Jerusalem."

"Do not tempt me," Asahel replied. "All my travels have carried me only to Jerusalem, and I find your plan inviting, even when I know that I cannot accept."

"Certainly one day more can make no difference."

"It will make much difference, my daughter," someone interrupted.

Miriam turned, startled by the voice. She had not noticed that her father rode behind them.

"It is dangerous, even now, for Asahel to be here. Rather, he should be riding with all haste to join the armies of Zedekiah."

Asahel nodded. "It would be most unfortunate if I should meet up with the armies of Nebuchadnezzar."

Miriam's smile faded as he spoke. "I'm sorry. It was selfish of me to forget."

"Sometimes it can be dangerous to forget, my daughter.

You are going far from home, where things will be very different and often puzzling."

"She will be among friends, Simeon," Asahel observed.

"Aye, but she must not forget that she is in the land of the enemy." Simeon sighed deeply. "I fear that not all the people of Babylon are as kind and friendly as Nebuzaradan and his nephew Urusar."

Miriam frowned and wondered just what kind of reception she would receive, even in the house of Nebuzaradan. "I will not forget," she said slowly, "but I am certain that there will be friendship between me and Urusar's sister Abilath."

For a short distance the road narrowed to little more than a strip of path between jagged rocks. The animals passed through in single file. One of the armed men took the bridle of Miriam's donkey and led it, so that it would not stumble and throw her down onto the rocks. Then the path widened once more and Asahel took his place beside her. Miriam looked up at him and smiled. "How I wish you could all come with me! When I return, I will tell you of all the things I have seen, so that you may share a part of it with me."

"I once heard a trader tell of a fabulous garden which Nebuchadnezzar has built for his Median wife," Asahel remarked. "It is said that he built it to represent a tiny mountain. Ever since I first heard of it, I have wondered about it."

"I will remember the garden and note it well," Miriam promised.

"Most likely it is a temple dedicated to one of their many gods. Enter it not, my daughter," Simeon warned, "for what has a daughter of Judah to do with the temples of idolatry?" Having expressed his conviction on this matter, Simeon said nothing further about it.

24

After hours of travel, the party arrived at the place where Simeon was to start his return home, and Miriam with her traveling companions was to meet and join the caravan of the prince Samgar-nebo, bound for Babylon.

The sun was almost directly overhead when Anak drew near and announced, "The time has come." Responding almost immediately, Simeon embraced his daughter, then stood looking down at her for a moment. "When the time is right, I will send for you," he said as she turned away to join the oncoming caravan. She brushed away her tears. From time to time she turned to wave until, at last, she could see him no longer. The fact that Asahel, Anak, and Leah were with her helped to sweeten a little the bitter grief of parting.

It was a strangely enchanting day. Miriam would never have believed the world could be so beautiful, or that anyone could be as happy as she was — after that first sadness of farewell had passed. Even the rocks and crags took on a shimmering loveliness in the clear fall air.

And never had she known Asahel as she learned to know him now. As they rode along, it seemed to Miriam as though she were riding away from childhood. She and Asahel did not scramble over the rocks in a wild game of tag, as they had done a few days before. They rode sedately, talking of the problems that lay ahead. She was amazed at Asahel's wisdom and proud that he felt her worthy of his confidences.

It was nearing sundown when they reached the inn where Miriam and Leah would spend the night. As the caravan came to a stop, Asahel leaned close to her and said softly, "I must now bid you good-by. I cannot rest here if I am to reach Jerusalem before morning."

"Can you not even stop long enough to take food with us?" Miriam asked in surprise.

He shook his head soberly, "No, I have already tarried

25

overlong." Turning on his heel, he was off. Miriam watched him stride down the road, hoping for a final gesture of farewell. There was none.

FIVE

The caravan was an imposing one. Samgar-nebo, prince of Babylon, was a man of power and wealth. His caravan included many slaves and beasts of burden, besides the armed men who strode at the front and rear to protect them.

Samgar-nebo rode near the head of the caravan, followed closely by his slaves and by the donkeys that bore the treasures that he had accumulated during his stay in Jerusalem. Behind these, Anak had placed the litter which Nebuzaradan had supplied for Miriam's comfort. In front of her litter were two Babylonian soldiers; behind it were two of her father's armed men and the beasts that carried her possessions and the gifts to the household of Nabuzaradan. At the far rear was the caravan of a merchant who had joined them for the protection that the Babylonian soldiers might offer.

It was now two days since they had joined the caravan. Miriam tried to relax in the cool shadow of her litter. A breeze rippled the curtains; Leah fastened them back to permit a clearer view of the countryside.

Miriam sighed and tried to ignore the cloud of dust that swirled up around them, raised by the many feet that had gone ahead. For a while Anak had permitted her to ride outside the litter. That was before the rumbling had begun, before Samgar-nebo had ordered the caravan to leave the road and go up into the hills among the rocks.

"I guess that I shall never truly be a lady," Miriam fretted to Leah. "Did Samgar-nebo say why we must ride inside the litter?"

"He said nothing, but at the cooking fire last night I heard it said the chariots of Nebuchadnezzar would soon pass by. If that is true, we will be safer inside."

"The danger will be small enough, and we could see them coming from miles away," Miriam countered. "Perhaps if I asked Anak, he would permit us to ride outside again."

"No, Miriam! You forget that Anak is not the master of this caravan. Would you make us such a burden that Samgar-nebo deserts us?"

The rumbling sound had become louder. The very earth seemed to tremble as they hurried up the steep, rough road. An order to halt was passed back through the caravan. The litter was lowered to the ground behind a huge rock that nearly shut off their view of the plains below.

The two girls leaned close together and peered from between the curtains. Suddenly it was as though the very grains of sand on the plains below had taken shape and begun to move. Leah nudged Miriam and said something, but Miriam could hear nothing but the pounding hoofs of many horses and the screech and whine of hundreds of stone wheels turning.

A sea of billowing dust rolled up toward them. "Quick, Leah! The curtains!" Miriam exclaimed, frantically tucking in the one nearest her. She could see the men unwinding their turbans or pulling their head scarves across their faces.

Miriam could scarcely breathe. She could taste the dust on her lips and feel the grit between her teeth. She wound her scarf tightly about her head and face and crouched down, burying her face in a cushion. But nothing could

27

shut out the dust or deafen her ears to the terrifying sound of Nebuchadnezzar's chariots.

After what seemed to be hours the sound began to fade. Miriam could hear the voices of the men, but she made no move. Leah tapped her shoulder. "Are you all right?" she asked.

"I am all right, but I intend to stay right here until that horrid old dust has settled." Miriam's voice came muffled through the cushion.

They were moving again. The bearers were grumbling loudly. One of them stumbled and the girls were nearly thrown from the litter. In the shouting that followed, Miriam sat up and swung her legs over the edge and stepped to the ground.

Anak hurried to where she stood. "Are you hurt?" he asked.

Miriam shook her head and looked about in surprise. The path was steep and very rocky. The bearer who had stumbled groaned loudly.

"No wonder they complain!" she said and added hopefully, "would it not be better if Leah and I again rode outside? There is little dust now."

"No, we are forced to the higher road that we may travel without being molested by the foot soldiers who will soon be passing below. Even so, we cannot be certain that they will not see us and loot our train."

"Would the soldiers of Babylon dare to molest Samgarnebo?"

"These soldiers must loot and plunder for food. I think they would care little who it was they robbed, be it the barn and house of some Judean farmer or the caravan of a Babylonian prince."

Seeing her worried frown, he added, "But I think that there is little enough reason for worry, for we will soon reach the village where we will spend the night at an inn. There our goods will be hidden away."

"Nay," one of the Babylonian guards corrected him, "we will reach no inn this night. A messenger has only now arrived warning Samgar-nebo that the soldiers are in the town, rioting and looting. We will travel until darkness falls, then camp among the rocks. If all goes well, no one will notice us."

Evening was already laying long shadows among the rocks when the order to halt was passed back through the caravan. The litter was lowered, and Miriam and Leah stepped out to ease their stiff, cramped muscles. As Miriam watched the men set up camp for the night, Leah hurried off to the one meager cooking fire.

They had not finished eating their meal when one of the guards scattered the fire and beat out the embers, leaving the camp in darkness. "I cannot see to eat," Miriam fretted. "Yet, I know it is for our own protection that the camp be hidden by night."

Miriam shivered in the chill darkness. An uneasy silence had settled over the camp. "We are a big caravan and have many armed men," she said impatiently, "still, Samgar-nebo fears attack."

"I think he would not have given such an order if it was a useless one," was Leah's comment.

It seemed to Miriam that she had scarcely closed her eyes when she was terrified by riotous shouting in the camp. She realized instantly that the camp was under attack. Cautiously she crept to the door of her tent and peered out.

In the bright moonlight she could see that the fighting was centered in the foremost section of the camp, where Samgar-nebo and his servants were quartered. Then she saw a man with a torch slipping past the fighting group and making his way toward her tent. Anak and her father's guards quickly stepped in front of him.

"Come, Miriam! We must hide!" Leah grasped her arm and drew her away from the opening.

"Where would you hide, Leah? There is no place where he could not find us."

"Out behind the rocks! They are too busy to notice our going!"

"Do not fret, Leah. We are in no danger. The men will drive him back."

But Anak and the armed men could not drive the man away, for it seemed that he was not alone. Anak had backed up until he stood before the entrance of the tent. Raising his arms in a gesture of pleading, he cried, "In the name of Jehovah, do not harm her. She is but a child."

"You are a Judean?" the man asked in surprise. "A Judean, traveling in the company of a Babylonian?"

"Aye. Anak, the servant of Simeon, taking my master's daughter to a haven of safety. I but travel with this caravan for added safety, as does the merchant who follows us."

"Out of the way, old man." The man roughly elbowed Anak aside. He tore away the curtain door and thrust his torch inside.

Leah covered her face, whimpering with fear. Miriam watched her, too frightened to move or to cry out. At sight of the scowling face behind the torch her fear turned to anger. "Are you not ashamed of yourself?" she demanded.

She turned and put a protecting arm about Leah's shoulders. "It must make you very proud to know that you have frightened Leah and made her cry!"

The strange man let out a whoop of laughter. "She must be a daughter of Judah," he called to his companions outside the tent, "for no pampered Babylonian maid would have such spirit!"

30

"Peace go with you." At these words the torch was suddenly extinguished and the intruder disappeared.

In a moment another man was standing at the entrance and asking, "Where is he? I but now saw his torch and heard his laughter." It was the leader of the Babylonian guards.

Miriam looked up at him, bewildered by the sudden change. "I do not know," she gasped. "Only an instant ago he stood where you now stand. I did not see him go.

"Who was he?" Leah asked.

"A leader of thieves! While some of his men held us in battle, others carried off Samgar-nebo's chests. Now they are gone!" The guard paused, scratching the back of his head. "I don't mind telling you that Samgar-nebo is exceedingly angry. He may ask why it is that your goods have been so little damaged."

"You are saying that he will believe that they were our friends? I assure you, they were not! He attacked us also, and my servant is badly hurt." Anak groaned loudly in the darkness behind her, and Leah spoke softly, comforting him.

"If our goods have not been taken, it is you who have saved us. Was it not your coming that drove him away?"

"What of your own armed men?" he asked Miriam.

"I know not, except that they were fighting at the entrance of my tent, and now they are gone."

"I will search for them."

Miriam reached out quickly and touched his arm. "Thank you. You are most kind to us." As he paused, she slipped a wide golden bracelet from her arm and held it toward him. He took it, examined it briefly, grunted his satisfaction, and was gone.

Miriam knelt down beside Anak and asked softly, "Are you hurt badly?"

"No, little one," he whispered, "I was but knocked to

the ground with a bump on the head, but they must not think we suffered too lightly. Come, Leah, bind my head well, that all may see how I suffer."

SIX

Day followed day in an ever-changing pattern, as their road wound through the plains and over the hills. There were days when they rode through a countryside dotted with orchards of olive, fig, or pomegranate, or the sweeping fields where grain would grow in the spring. On other days they passed vineyards growing on terraced hillsides or rocky barren hills where only an occasional wild plant could exist.

Miriam was amazed to find that the world was so large. She had often heard her father speaking to Anak of far places, but distances mean little to one who has never been farther than a few miles from home.

The day was unseasonably warm after the cold winds and rain of the day before. Miriam lay back lazily against the cushions, lulled by the swaying rhythm of the litter. She was roused by Leah's voice saying, "We are near a city, Miriam."

"What city?" Miriam asked, suddenly wide awake. "Think you that we will stop for a time and, perhaps, even visit the bazaar?"

"I know not what city it is. The men at the cooking fires were surly and little given to talk. Samgar-nebo grows more impatient; every day he drives both men and beasts until the men speak of little else."

Miriam sat up and peered through the curtains of the litter. There was no visible sign to indicate that they neared a city. She could see only the peaceful countryside rimmed by the distant blue-gray mountains. It was not until high noon that they saw the city.

"Cities are exciting places," Miriam mused as she looked in delight at the houses and shops.

Leah nodded. "Yet there is a strangeness in each that I do not like. Always I have lived among people and things which I knew well. I see too many strange things here and they frighten me."

"Poor Leah, you are missing half of the fun!"

Leah smiled and listened as Miriam chattered on. After a time she sat up and parted the curtains a little to glance out. In consternation she quickly drew her head back. She sat silent, swaying slowly back and forth, folding and unfolding her hands.

"What on earth ails you?" Miriam cried in alarm.

"We are alone," Leah sobbed. "Of all the caravan, only our litter bearers and two guards have left the broad road."

Miriam looked cautiously through the curtains and found that what Leah had said was true. She felt cold and, although the day was warm, she shivered. She had a sudden desire to huddle down into the corner and cover her face to shut out the strangeness of the sights and sounds around her. But she knew that she must remain calm and that she must comfort Leah. She licked her lips and forced them into a smile. "Do not be alarmed, Leah," she said soothingly. "It is not likely that our armed men would have taken us from the caravan without orders. Perhaps Samgar-nebo plans to rest here for a day, and we but go apart to some inn."

She moved so that she could lay an arm about Leah's thin shoulders. "Anak has promised my father that he will protect us. Even if he does not, we know that he is a good man and loves us both well. He would never desert us in a strange city."

Leah dried her eyes and drew away. "You are right, but why did we not go to the same inn as the rest?"

"I too have been wondering," Miriam admitted. "Perhaps we were sent this way because Samgar-nebo had reason to fear that they might meet with some trouble in the street ahead."

Leah began to sob again. "Do not cry, Leah, but think! Did you overhear the men saying anything, this morning, that would lead you to think that we might be stopping in this city for a time?"

Leah shook her head. "I heard nothing — except that we drew near to a city." She paused, wiping her eyes on the corner of her scarf. "Samgar-nebo is already irked by the slowness of our travel and the men grow surly and hard to manage. He would know that if he stopped here they might run away, or drink overmuch wine."

"Do not worry about that," Miriam said. She was surprised at the sharpness of her tone. More gently she added, "Both Anak and Samgar-nebo are men used to handling other men. They will have considered well whatever they plan to do. We must trust them."

It was a strange, new experience for Miriam to be quieting another's fears. Always before, she had been the one who was comforted. It gave her a pleasant sense of power and strength. But why was it, she wondered, that while her words seemed to convince Leah, she could not completely convince herself? She felt the old rebellion rising up within her: why had she been born a girl? If she had been a boy, she would have known whether or not this was all part of the plan.

The bearers stopped and the litter was lowered. Leah

peered cautiously through the curtains, but Miriam quickly swung her legs to the ground. As she stood up, she drew her scarf across her face. She was standing in the courtyard of an inn. "What are we doing here?" she demanded of one of the guards.

He made no answer, only shrugged, as he turned and strode to the inn door and shouted. "Anna!" he called.

A short, plump little lady hurried out in answer to his call. He motioned to where Miriam stood and said, "The daughter of Simeon."

"I am Anna," the woman explained as she put an arm about Miriam's waist and led her into the inn.

Miriam looked around the room. Her travels had taught her that this was not the usual accommodation offered by a small inn. She was aware that this must be the family room of the innkeeper and his wife. She looked up to find Anna watching her.

"Peace be unto you," Anna said smiling. "You honor our poor house."

"May Jehovah bless you and your household for your kindnesses, most gracious lady," Miriam answered politely.

A servant entered, bringing fruit and bread and a savory stew of lamb for their midday meal. Anna moved busily about, seeing to it that they were served. Then she sat down beside Miriam and said, "Anak is an old friend to this house. He has often stopped here when he traveled abroad on his master's business."

Miriam picked gingerly at the food which had been set before her. She felt no hunger, only weariness edged with a sickening tinge of insecurity. "What will Samgar-nebo do when he finds that we are not with the caravan?" she fretted. "He is already angry that we have slowed his progress."

"That is why you are here," Anna assured them.

"You mean that he has gone on without us?" Leah cried.

"Nay, nay, worry not yourselves. Samgar-nebo will also rest here through the heat of this day, that he may travel faster and for longer hours later. Even now Anak is dickering with a camel trader, trying to exchange your litter and its bearers for a camel equipped to carry you."

"But why did Anak not tell us of this?"

"Because there was no need," someone interrupted.

Miriam turned, startled by the voice. Anak, who was standing in the doorway, continued. "The decision was between Samgar-nebo and me, and I acted upon it."

"We were frightened!"

"Why should you have been? Has not your father charged me with your safety? Does not Nebuzaradan hold Samgar-nebo responsible for your safe delivery to his house?"

Miriam could find no answer to his rebuke. When she made no reply, he added, "Anna will show you a place where you may rest. I would advise that you sleep while you can, for from now on there will be little time for rest."

In the days that followed, Miriam remembered Anak's words, for Samgar-nebo drove the men and animals from early morning until after sundown. They traveled through sunny days and days when the chill winds blew out of the north, sharp with rain. Much of the country through which they now passed was barren and rocky.

Whenever it was possible, they stopped for the night at an inn, but when no such facility was available, they set up camp, and then the lights of their cooking fires flared through the darkness of a deserted place.

As the days went by Miriam often said, "I am glad that you are the one my father chose to go with me."

"Aye, the trip would have been overhard for one of Deborah's age," Leah would answer. She knew full well that this was not what Miriam meant, but discretion decreed that she must speak so.

36

They fought the monotony of their days with storytelling and singing, and playing old games and inventing new ones.

One day Samgar-nebo left his place at the head of the caravan to ride back along its entire length. As he approached Miriam and Leah, he heard them laughing and turned his horse to ride beside them. "It is good to find you in such happy spirits," he said. "I wish that the rest could find something to laugh about."

"We were playing a game," Miriam explained.

"And did I not also hear a harp and singing?"

Miriam nodded. "We know many songs. Sometimes we make up new ones."

In thoughtful silence he rode beside them for a time. Then he turned and said, "I have a young servant girl named Islah. She is about your age and finds her days exceedingly dull. Would not the companionship of another help to shorten your day, even as it would shorten hers? I do not doubt that she knows many stories and at least a few new games and songs. May I send her to join you?"

"Please do! I am sure that we can make room for another if we sit close."

Samgar-nebo smiled and saluted in farewell. He reined his horse around and continued on his way to the rear of the caravan.

It was during the noon rest on the following day that the girl first joined them. As she climbed up, she turned and spoke to the man who had accompanied her. The words were strange and the sound of them puzzled Miriam.

When their greetings had been said, and Islah settled between the two, she turned to Miriam and said shyly, "It is kind of you to let me join you. I only hope that my presence here will shorten your day as much as I know it will shorten mine."

Miriam smiled happily. "It will be great fun, Islah."

Then she sobered. "When you spoke to that man, I could not understand your words. I had not considered that my tongue would not be understood in the household of Nebuzaradan — or their words understood by me."

"I will teach both you and Leah," Islah offered eagerly. "Then, when you reach the house of your friend, you will understand."

"Miriam will learn quickly, but I am stupid as a donkey. I shall try hard, but I fear I can never learn." Leah's forehead wore a worried frown.

The girls laughed, but Islah reassured Leah, "Do not fear; if you try, you will learn."

Islah spent part of each day with them. Soon they had learned many new and strange-sounding words. They chatted in a language which was half Judean and half Babylonian.

"See, even as I said, you have learned quickly!" Islah announced happily.

"Indeed," Miriam agreed, "even our little donkey!" She gave Leah a friendly nudge, and Leah smiled with pleasure.

SEVEN

Miriam breathed deeply of the fresh, clear morning air as she stepped out into the courtyard of the inn. "It will be a fair day," Anak remarked as he helped her climb up into the litter on the back of the kneeling camel.

"Aye," she agreed happily, for as Leah took her place beside her, Miriam could see Islah hurrying to join them.

38

The camel objected to the heavy load, but the driver only laughed. He had kept the reins tight so that the beast could not snap at Islah's heels as she clambered up.

"My master said that I might spend the whole day with you," Islah said, settling herself.

"Up!" The camel driver commanded.

The camel balked and made no move to rise.

"Up, you miserable, mangy creature!" the driver ordered again, jerking the lead rope and prodding the camel with the sharp stick he carried.

Still whining and complaining, the camel struggled to her feet. The girls laughed and the camel turned her head to look back at them in a haughty manner.

"You must not laugh at Murah," the driver chided, "for she is most unhappy. Rather, why do you not sing to her, that she may forget her troubles?"

"Have you so soon forgotten that she does not like our singing?" Miriam asked.

"It is even as our lady says, our singing does not please the sensitive ears of Murah," Islah agreed, smiling down at him. "Rather, it is your own singing that gives wings to her heavy feet."

He nodded, greatly flattered. "You speak with truth and wisdom. It is I who will sing for her."

A shout to start moving rang back through the caravan. As they set off, the camel driver began his song. It was a strange wordless chant, sung in a shrill, nasal voice. Leah put her hands over her ears and wrinkled her nose in distaste, and the others nodded in agreement. But the camel perked her ears and stepped quickly along, well pleased by what she heard.

The sun was nearing its zenith when word was passed back announcing the approach of another caravan. As it came abreast, both caravans halted. All along the way the

39

armed men bared their weapons and stood ready, in case of trouble.

The girls peered from between the lowered curtains as Anak and Samgar-nebo, along with their armed men, walked to meet the leaders of the other caravan. They spoke together, then returned to their own caravans.

The strange caravan moved on, but the men of Samgar-nebo's caravan clustered about their leader to hear the news. A great shout arose. "They must have brought us great news," Miriam mused.

"Perhaps it is that our journey nears its end," Islah said. She smiled mysteriously.

Leah nodded. "This morning I heard rumors of such a possibility."

"And you told me nothing?" Miriam said it with a chiding inflection.

"I would not raise your hopes, only to have you disappointed," Leah replied.

The camel driver returned. Leah folded back the curtain and leaned out to ask, "They brought good news?"

"Oh, yes, they certainly did bring good news!" the driver exclaimed. "They assure us that it is still possible that we may reach the gates of Babylon before sundown." Turning to the camel, he cried, "Come, Murah, my lovely one! Lift your dainty feet high and set them back down quickly! Move swiftly, O beautiful one, and this night you will know the luxury that is Babylon!"

The caravan was on its way again and the happiness of the men was loud in their laughter as they shouted to one another. Even the animals seemed to sense that they neared the end of their journey and hurried eagerly forward.

From her high perch, Miriam noticed a man riding swiftly away. Islah saw him too and said, "See, there goes the messenger of Samgar-nebo. He will be carrying a mes-

40

sage to the men who stand guard at the outer gate, instructing them to hold their gates open in case we should not arrive before the setting of the sun."

"Think you that they will heed his request?" Miriam asked in surprise.

Islah nodded. "Oh, yes, Samgar-nebo is a prince of Babylon and a favorite of Nebuchadnezzar. They will wait."

Though the caravan traveled at a faster than usual pace, it was midafternoon before they could dimly see the great city. It was nearing sundown when shouts from the head of the caravan announced that the outer walls and a few other landmarks were clearly visible, but darkness had settled before they halted at one of the hundred bronze gates. There was much shouting and the flare of many torches as the guards, marching up and down, were inspecting the caravan.

Servants of the merchant began setting up their camp for another night outside the gates, for only the caravan of Samgar-nebo was allowed entrance at so late an hour.

The road along which they now traveled was darkened by the shadow of the largest buildings that Miriam had ever seen. Islah proudly explained, "Is it not a fine array of buildings that Nebuchadnezzar has built to house the men of our great army? Soon now, sweet Miriam, we will pass through the gate of Ishtar and down the street of temples. I wish that I could have shown Babylon to you at midday. Then you would have seen her true beauty. Now you will see only the shadows of her greatness. See, already we near the great lion that guards the way."

Outside the gate called after the goddess Ishtar the caravan paused again. When the camel knelt, Islah dismounted and said, "I must leave you here. May the gods ever walk before you."

Before Miriam realized that the time of parting had

come, Islah was already hurrying away. "Jehovah go with you," Miriam called after her.

Miriam could not see the great structure when they passed the Hanging Gardens and the palace of Nebuchadnezzar. Nor did she notice that her caravan had left the broad street of the temples and the market section behind, for all was bathed in darkness. It seemed that they traveled on endlessly, following the bobbing torches of the guards.

Suddenly there was a signal to halt. An armed guard pounded against the outer gate of a house. A voice from inside called, "Go away! The household has retired for the night and your noise disturbs their slumbers."

"Open!" the guard ordered. "It is the caravan of Samgar-nebo, prince of Babylon, who wishes to deliver to you a guest of the house of Nebuzaradan — one Miriam, daughter of Simeon, and her servants."

There was the clanking sound of chains being loosened, and slowly the gate swung open. Their camel was commanded to kneel. Miriam and Leah stepped slowly down and into the courtyard of the house of Nebuzaradan.

A maid bearing a lamp came into the yard to welcome them and to conduct them into the house. Then she led them down a long hall to a room where many lamps burned. Miriam looked about her with pleasure. It was the most beautiful room that she had ever seen. Shining hangings draped the walls of brightly decorated glazed tile. There were luxurious couches and furnishings with gold and pearl inlays. In the center of the room was a pool where bright fish swam.

"At last you have come!" said a gentle voice.

The startled Miriam wheeled about and saw a tiny, doll-like girl resting on a couch behind her. Walking slowly toward her, Miriam greeted her. "You must be the lady Abilath," she said, smiling down at her.

42

"And you are Miriam. I have heard so many things concerning you. Oh, Miriam! I thought that you would never get here! And now that you are here, it is much too late for a long, friendly talk. Besides, you are travel-worn and much in need of rest."

EIGHT

Miriam awoke slowly, luxuriating in the softness of the couch on which she lay and enjoying the fragrant incense in the air she breathed. She opened her eyes slowly, but the glare of light that she had expected was not there. The sunlight came softly through the tinted hangings that covered the windows. She stretched and was pleased to find that the stiff soreness of travel had left her body.

"I thought that you would never awaken," Abilath remarked softly.

Abilath sat on a long, low chair beside the pool. She turned and rested her chin on the palm of her hand as she watched Miriam.

"Have I slept so very late? Why did you not awaken me?"

"You slept so soundly. Indeed, Hannah and I moved most quietly so as not to awaken you."

"How kind of you!" Miriam walked to Abilath's chair and sat down near her on the low wall that edged the pool.

"I have been told many things about you," Abilath said softly. "But never did I think that you would be so fair to look upon. Urusar said your hair was like the setting sun, but he did not tell me that you were a golden goddess."

Miriam laughed in surprised pleasure at the exaggerated

43

compliment. "Thank you, Abilath. Always Asahel has teased me about the color of my hair and I have envied Leah her black braids."

They both laughed. There was no reason for laughing except a sudden burst of joy in their new-found friendship.

Hannah heard their laughter and came to join them. When she drew the hangings back from the windows, bright sunlight filled the room. "You look much rested, my child," she noted.

"May I show her the garments which we have made for her?" Abilath coaxed.

Hannah nodded. "I will call Merab that she may bring them while Leah is preparing Miriam for the day." Turning to Miriam, she added, "It is not that we thought your own raiment would not be fitting but rather that in these first days they might be in need of freshening."

"How thoughtful you both are." Miriam paused, suddenly feeling shy. "Most of what I have has become faded and shabby with travel and will need to be replaced from the materials my father sent with me. He said that you would know how they should be fashioned. There is enough in each piece so that Abilath shall have one, too."

Hannah smiled. "Your father is a wise man, Miriam. Wise and generous."

Merab brought the garments and laid them out for Miriam to see. The material was rich and fine, and there were two sets of everything.

"There is one of the same shade of blue as the one I am wearing," Abilath began eagerly.

"Hush, little one. You must let her choose for herself," Hannah chided gently.

"Oh, but the blue is my choice for today." Miriam assured them. She lifted the garment, holding it against

44

her. Never had she owned such a robe. The material was thin and soft, with a wide strip of embroidery encircling the hem and neck and a large clip at the shoulder.

Leah set a bowl of fruit on a table where Miriam could reach it. She hummed softly as she rubbed the sweet-smelling oils into Miriam's skin and helped her to dress in the new clothing.

"You seem to be pleased with the morning, Leah," Miriam teased. "I think that you are happy in this house."

"Oh, yes, Miriam," Leah replied. "I am treated with great kindness, and already I have found two good friends in Merab and Hannah."

Flushing shyly, she paused and glanced to where Hannah was coaxing Abilath to eat. "While we waited for you to awaken, Hannah told me that Anak had instructed her to find me a husband from among our people here — it was my father's wish. She also said that the good Simeon has provided me with a handsome dowry, in payment of my services to you."

"Oh, Leah, I do hope that Hannah will find someone who will please you well!"

"Aye," Leah answered, blushing, "already she thinks that she knows of such a one."

Miriam glanced to where Hannah stood and found that she was watching them. "I would be most honored to find a husband for Miriam also, should her father desire it."

"Oh no!" Leah interrupted. "My lady has been betrothed for many years to Asahel, son of Caleb. Their wedding day will bring great joy to both their houses."

Hannah smiled and nodded. "That is as it should be."

"I will soon be of an age that my uncle will be seeking a husband for me also." Abilath remarked happily. Then she paused, and the smile faded from her face as she looked from one to the other. "But, then," she added bitterly, "it

45

is not likely that any man would willingly take to wife a girl who is a cripple."

"Do not grieve yourself, my pretty one," Hannah comforted her. "There are many who, could they but know you, would vie for your hand because of your goodness and for your beauty's sake."

"We will make you walk!" Miriam cried impulsively. "We will live together and do all of the things that will make you well and strong again."

"Already I feel better, and who can say how soon I will walk?"

Pash, the huge black eunuch, came and carried Abilath out into the garden, to the place where her swinging couch stood. Miriam followed and sat down on a stone bench beside her, watching as Merab pulled at the heavy cord that swung the couch slowly back and forth.

Abilath was in a happy mood. She laughed as she settled herself comfortably on her cushions. "When my uncle told me about you," she said, "I felt as though I knew you well. Oh, Miriam, it is just as I have so often dreamed that it would be!" Then, as always when she spoke impulsively, she flushed with embarrassment. "Urusar laughed at me when I insisted that I already knew you. Perhaps you will laugh also."

"Nay," Miriam assured her quickly, "for I have also felt that I knew you. Urusar told me many things about you. I doubt that he would have noticed me in the first place if the sight of me had not reminded him of you."

The smile faded from Abilath's face as Miriam spoke, and an expression of sadness settled in its place. "The house is cruelly empty when the men are gone. Each time they return, I hope that it is to stay — but always they must leave again. Why are there so many wars to be fought? I hate war!"

"But the wars have scarcely touched you here," Miriam answered. "It is far different in my land."

Abilath bit her lower lip, an impulsive gesture which did not go unnoticed.

"I am sorry if I have offended you," Miriam said quickly. "I know how lonely it must be for you when Urusar and the great Nebuzaradan are gone. Yet, your home has suffered no damage, and you may still sit here in your own beautiful garden." Her eyes began to swim with tears of sudden homesickness. She looked down so that Abilath would not notice, and then she continued, "For many years my land has been a battleground. Jeremiah says that it is our punishment."

"Punishment? Then you have angered your gods?" Abilath asked in shocked surprise.

"Aye, our nation has sinned. Our leaders have turned away from Jehovah, and there are many who follow in their ways. They will not listen to Jeremiah."

"So your god is angry and sends my king and his armies to destroy you." Abilath lay back in silent thought. Then she added, "It is impossible for me to understand the ways of the gods, but this I know: yesterday I was lonely, but today you are here and we are friends.

"Tell me of your home, Miriam. Urusar has told me of Judah, but he likes not the country and finds little joy in telling of it."

"It is a beautiful country!" Miriam asserted in quick defense.

Abilath laughed. "I would expect that you would think so. That is why I want to hear of it from your lips. You see, I have been curious to know what it really is like."

Miriam thought for a moment. "It is a land rich in vineyards and flocks, but not so rich as it once was. Many of our people have already been carried into exile."

"And what of Jerusalem? Is it big and beautiful, like our city?"

"I have never seen Jerusalem, and it is little of your city that I saw as I passed through it in the night."

"Of course, it is not as beautiful as Babylon! Everyone knows that Jerusalem is no more than a collection of mud huts within a wall!"

The bitterness that might have developed from further exchanges was suddenly interrupted by the arrival of a girl who stopped in the doorway. She was beautifully gowned and wore many jeweled bracelets on her arms. The late afternoon sun set her all aglitter, and there were glints of light in her shining black hair. Bells tinkled at her ankles as she walked toward them.

"Yaama!" Abilath gasped. "What a pleasure!"

Yaama nodded, but her eyes never left Miriam as she studied her from the top of her head to the gold-embroidered sandals that Abilath had given her. "I heard that Nebuzaradan had sent you an Israelite, and I thought I would come and see her."

"How kind! Miriam, this is Lady Yaama."

Miriam smiled up at the girl. She was not prepared for the look of hard anger which she received, or the sharp words. "It seems that your new slave has not been properly trained! If she were mine, I would have her beaten for her insolence!"

"No, Yaama!" Abilath exclaimed in surprise. "She is not a slave, but a guest in the house of Nebuzaradan."

"If it pleases you to pretend while you are alone with her, it makes no difference to me, but I shall expect her to show me the proper respect." She paused and looked down at Abilath. Then she added, "How can I say what I would do if I were in your condition? Still, I do not think it wise that you treat her as an equal."

"Why will you not understand?" Abilath asked impatiently.

"Do you expect me to believe that Nebuzaradan seeks his friends in the households of the enemy?" Yaama demanded. She turned scornfully to where Miriam sat and studied her for a time before adding, "How can you be certain that she is not a spy, or an assassin who will kill you while you sleep?"

Miriam flushed and lifted her chin proudly. "I know not what Lady Yaama is willing to believe concerning me. I am sorry that she finds my presence here not to her liking, but this much I must say: this household will suffer no evil at my hands."

"Silence!" Yaama commanded sharply, stamping her foot. Turning to Abilath she demanded, "Why do you sit there silent, allowing this insolent daughter of the scum of Judah to . . . to . . ."

"Will you not even give Miriam a chance to defend herself?" Abilath interrupted her angrily.

"I have no interest in what she may say, for I know what I know and it is this: Nebuzaradan would not have sent her here, nor would she have come, except as the plunder of war."

Miriam looked from one to the other. Could it be that what Yaama said was true? Nay, it could not be! Surely her father would have told her if he had made such an agreement with Nebuzaradan. Yet, she realized that she knew nothing of what had passed between them.

"You can have her for friend if you wish," Yaama was saying. "As for me, I hate all things Judean. They are a weak nation, born for slavery. I trust them not, for they are a tricky lot."

"How can you say that when Nebuchadnezzar himself has placed them in positions of trust?"

Yaama shrugged. "And who can say that they will not return his kindness by rising against him?" She waved scornfully toward Miriam. "Take her for friend if you are such a fool, but slave she is, and do not expect me to treat her otherwise."

"Whatever you may think," Abilath said quietly, "she is guest in this house and a dear friend of Nebuzaradan's."

The color had drained from Yaama's cheeks, but not the anger from her eyes. She looked thoughtfully from one girl to the other, before asking, "And Urusar's friend also?"

Abilath answered coldly, "It was Urusar who first told me about her."

Yaama turned without a word and left the garden. When she was gone, Abilath began to weep hysterically. "Why did she have to come and spoil our day?" she demanded.

Merab dropped the cord of the swing-chair and ran to summon Hannah.

Miriam knelt beside the couch and put her arms about Abilath. "It doesn't matter, Abilath, do not cry."

"It does matter!" Abilath sobbed. "She has insulted you and she must apologize! I will make my uncle demand that she apologize! I will send him a message telling him all that she said!"

"Nay, nay, Abilath, you are upsetting yourself. Yaama was unkind because she did not understand. It will do me no good if you anger her further. Perhaps it will be best if, in the future, I do not meet your friends. Others might also find our friendship hard to understand."

"Miriam is right." The two girls looked up to find that Hannah had joined them. "The friendship between Miriam and your uncle's household is one that many might not understand. To them, all Judeans are either the enemy at Jerusalem or servants, like me, brought back as plunder of war."

50

"But to me they're not . . ." Abilath began. Her voice faded away into the weakness that so often plagued her.

"Let us think no more about it," Miriam said with a smile which she hoped would hide the hurt and fears she felt. "I did not come here seeking Yaama's friendship, but only yours."

She stopped suddenly. What if Abilath believed those things which Yaama said, even as she herself had come to half believe them? She must know. "I am not a spy and you must believe that I will never hurt you," she blurted out.

Abilath laughed and threw her arms about her. "Of course, you are not! That much I know. Did I not tell you that I had known you for a long time?"

NINE

Merab entered the room and walked swiftly to where her mistress sat. "Lady Samilah approaches through the garden," she said softly.

"Do not let her wait, but show her in at once," Abilath ordered.

Abilath turned to Miriam and explained, "Samilah is the first and favorite wife of my uncle Nebuzaradan."

Samilah smiled as she entered the room. "Forgive me, my dear, I would have come sooner to meet your guest, but I wished to give you time to learn to know her first."

"Thank you, my lady," Abilath's smile told clearly that Samilah was one of her favorite people. "I was planning that we should visit you and Grandmother this very morning if you had not come. I seek your wisdom."

51

"My wisdom tells me that you are a happy child and that the companionship of your new friend is a priceless healing gift," Samilah said. More soberly she added, "It might be well, if you feel strong enough, to go this very day to the temples with gifts of thanks to the gods for her safe arrival."

Turning to Miriam, she said, "You are as lovely as I had heard you would be. How wise my husband was to bring you here, my dear."

Miriam smiled and bowed as Deborah had taught her. "My lady is most kind."

Samilah smiled. "I hope that you will always find kindness and happiness in this house."

"It is that of which I would speak, my lady," Abilath interrupted. She told of Yaama's visit and the unpleasant conversation that followed.

Samilah listened quietly. When Abilath had finished, she said, "I believe that Miriam and Hannah have spoken wisely. Yaama's anger will most quickly die if the act is forgotten. You must act as though it had never happened. Yet, in the future, we must never allow her the opportunity to insult Miriam again."

Abilath looked up in surprise. Samilah nodded. "I am as sorry as you are that Miriam has been so treated, but let us not dwell on unhappiness. The others also wait to meet your guest. The Old One is planning a party, with many foods and wine, in her honor. I have been instructed to invite you into our garden at sundown tomorrow."

"Oh, Samilah! And will the Egyptian dance?"

"If I tell you all that we have planned, there will be no surprises left," Samilah teased.

Miriam turned to Abilath, when Samilah had gone, and said, "She spoke of other women, yet I have seen no other since first I arrived."

52

"There are others," Abilath assured her. "Because of my illness, my uncle has kept me apart in my own rooms. There is Grandmother, who is Nebuzaradan's mother, and my father's mother also. Then there is Samilah, whom you have already met, and a young wife and other women. There are other children, too, but they are all much younger than I.

"Samilah visits me often, as does the Old One, and when I feel strong enough, I sometimes join them in their rooms." Abilath paused, smiling at the puzzled expression on Miriam's face. "How many women are there in your father's household?"

"My father has but one wife," Miriam replied, "and that is my mother. There are the servants, of course. I have a nurse named Deborah, but she is Anak's wife."

"How odd."

"Nay, my child," Hannah said, laughing, "it is but one of the many differences that you will find in the customs of your people and those of Miriam's."

Abilath shrugged. Then, forgetting everything except the party, she said softly, "I wonder whether the Egyptian will dance. I am certain that you have never seen anything to compare with it — yet, it reminds me of the moon as it weaves in and out of the clouds on stormy nights." So began Abilath's enjoyment of the party. It was like her, as Miriam was to find out through the months to come. Always Abilath enjoyed each little outing, first in anticipation, then the event itself, and finally, through endless hours of reliving it.

The girls were dressed with great care on the following evening. Leah spent much time in brushing perfume oils into Miriam's long red hair, as Hannah directed. At last it lay long and smooth about her shoulders.

"They may forget your name and your face," Hannah

53

remarked, as she stooped to arrange the folds of Miriam's outer garment beneath the heavy girdle, "but they will not forget your hair. Let other women adorn their heads with caps of gold net and jewels, but you must never wear one. You have no need for such."

Miriam nodded meekly, but she wanted to cry out that of all the things she had seen in Babylon, she came nearest to coveting the lovely cap of gold net that Merab was placing upon Abilath's black head.

At exactly sundown, Pash carried Abilath through a gate in the hedge. In the women's garden, tables and couches were set to the shape of a new moon before the wide arches that formed the entrance to the house. The light of many lamps glinted against the shiny faces of the leaves. From out of the shadows of a far corner, the thin high voice of a flute, accompanied by the deeper tones of a harp, floated out over the garden.

A withered old woman sat at the center of the table. She motioned to them to join her. Miriam stopped before the couch. This must be the Old One. She bowed low and said, as Hannah had directed her, "May Jehovah richly bless this house, for its loving kindness to the least one of His children."

The Old One smiled up at her with pleasure. "Sit here beside me," she said, "I would talk with you of many things."

Miriam returned her smile. She had feared meeting this old woman, knowing that here was the ruler of the women of the household. Yet, she should have known that the Old One would be kind, for everyone loved her.

After bowing low before both Samilah and the young wife and making the speeches she had been taught, Miriam took her place. As Leah arranged the folds of her robe, she watched Pash lowering Abilath to a place beside her.

Abilath turned toward her grandmother. "Your kind-

54

nesses to me are as many as the stars in the sky! How can I ever repay you?"

"I am more than repaid when I see your happiness, my little one. Tell me, is the pretty Miriam a magician? Or did Hannah paint that color in your cheeks?"

Miriam giggled. "It is the excitement, my lady. We have done nothing all day but plan for this hour."

"And you?" The Old One pointedly asked Miriam. "Are you happy in this house? Or do you find too great a longing for those you left behind?"

Miriam was silent for a moment, wondering how the Old One wished to be answered.

"You are homesick." The Old One nodded in sympathy.

"Oh, no, not any more," Miriam answered quickly. "Everyone has been so kind to me that I cannot be unhappy. The first days of my journey I knew a great loneliness, but that is all over now. Abilath and I are great friends, even as Urusar said that we would be."

"Ah, so you and Urusar are friends also." The Old One nodded and smiled, as though the thought pleased her. "And do you not think that my grandson is a handsome fellow?"

"Oh, yes, my lady," Miriam answered.

The Old One nodded again and turned to watch as servants entered, bearing bowls and platters of food.

The music of the flute and harp ceased. A young girl carrying a psaltery stepped from the women's hall and sat at one side of the great archway. "She is a Judean, like yourself," the grandmother remarked as the girl began her song. Miriam smiled back at her. It was a song that she knew well and a favorite of her father's. For a moment she could almost feel the cooling breezes of her own rooftop and the comfort of her father's presence.

"I do not understand the words," the Old One said softly,

"but I find the melody pleasing. Too often the music of your people has a melancholy sound. Of what does this song speak?"

"This one speaks of a maid's love for a young man," Miriam answered.

"And you? Have you chosen a young man to love?"

Miriam flushed uneasily under the questioning eyes of the woman. "A young man has been chosen for me," she answered.

The Old One sighed. "It was an old woman's dream that my grandson Urusar might be pleased to keep you here. It does not really matter. Tell me of this man who has been chosen for you."

With many such questions the Old One was drawing from Miriam the story of her home and those dear to her, until, with a loud clash of cymbals, the music again changed for the Egyptian dancer. Miriam was held spellbound, for she had never seen anything to compare with the strange undulating movements of the dance.

"It is a dance of praise to their great sun god, Ra," Abilath explained when it was over.

As the evening moved on, there were many changes of music and many dances. Some of the dancers came from the temple of Ishtar, some were slaves of the household. Miriam found it all very exciting, but Abilath grew weary and finally went to sleep on her couch.

Samilah made her way around the table to sit for a time beside Miriam, visiting with her. Then the young wife came and Miriam was surprised to find that she was no older than Leah. One by one they all came and spoke with her and with the Old One. When the last one had retired, the Old One motioned to Pash. "We will soon meet again," she said as the huge slave lifted Abilath from her couch.

She embraced Miriam, silencing the fine words of parting which Hannah had taught her. "Now to bed with you both, that tomorrow may not be completely lost in slumber," the Old One ordered, with a last affectionate pat.

TEN

It seemed to Miriam that she had scarcely fallen asleep when she was awakened. Abilath sat on the edge of her couch, slowly drawing cool fingers across her eyes.

"Shhh," Abilath warned softly. "Do not speak out or Hannah will hear you, and I would like to speak with you alone. We must plan our visit to the temples."

When Miriam made no answer, she added, "Today we must go to the temples and thank the gods for your safe journey, even as Samilah said."

"Today?" Miriam asked softly. She was filled with a sudden fear of hurting her friend's feelings. How could she make Abilath understand that she could not enter the temples of a false god?

Abilath went on happily, "Samilah warned me again last night that I must go, else we may offend them."

It was little comfort for Miriam to know that Hannah would not permit her to go. Somehow she must make Abilath understand. "Before I left my father's house," she began slowly, "he told me many things. One was that I must seek Hannah's guidance in all things, as to what our law will permit; another was that I must not ever enter your temples."

Abilath frowned, but Miriam hurried on, "Forgive me, Abilath, but I dare not enter."

"No, it is you who must forgive me! In my eagerness to show you the wonders of my city, I forgot. Hannah has warned me that I must never invite you to enter one of our temples. Please do not tell her that I forgot."

Miriam threw her arms around Abilath and hugged her. "Fear not, I will not tell."

Then, as her eyes rested on Abilath, she almost shouted in her surprise. "Abilath! How did you get to my bedside?"

Abilath, trying to conceal the thrill at her achievement, answered as calmly as she could, "I walked. Since I first heard that you were coming, I have known that I must walk. You must not tell the others, for they would never permit it."

"But why?"

"It is very painful for me to stand upon my feet, and they would say that it is a useless pain." Abilath puckered her face in imitation of Hanna's frown. "As you have seen, my leg does not want to straighten and my toe points in." She paused and sighed deeply as she inspected the crippled foot. "At first I just stood on my feet for a while, and sometimes it hurt me so badly that I cried. . . . O Miriam, I do so want to walk again!"

"I will help you."

Abilath got slowly to her feet, steadying herself against the couch. "Yes, now that you know, you can help me. It will make it much easier."

Miriam helped her back to the couch. As they walked slowly along, she resumed talking about Jewish taboos. "I cannot enter your temples, but maybe I can wait outside while you go in. We can ask Hannah. She will know whether I will anger Jehovah by doing so."

"What a bother!" Abilath objected, dropping down on

her couch. "Our gods care little how many other gods we worship, so long as we worship them also. And they care not what we eat, either."

Abilath's words reminded her that she must also ask Hannah concerning the foods, especially the meats. Certainly there could be nothing wrong with tasting the fragrant fowl roasted in wine, or the spiced lamb that dripped with honey. Yet she had not dared to taste either one, not even when the grandmother had urged her to do so. For, was there not always a danger that they had not been prepared according to the law?

"Hannah says that your god is a just god," Abilath's voice interrupted her thoughts, "but if he is so just, why does he punish the good people, like you and Hannah, along with the evil ones?"

"Hush!" Miriam cried, her voice sharp with fear. "You must not blaspheme the Most High! It is right that Judah should be punished, the just with the unjust. Our leaders do not listen to Jehovah's prophets, and our people have turned their backs on His laws and His teachings. Many of them worship false gods and even make sacrifices to them."

Abilath shrugged. "It is not important. Let it not come between us. You worship your Jehovah as you wish and I will worship my gods."

Miriam did not say the words which she was about to say. It was not right for her to let Abilath believe that Jehovah was harsh and unjust, yet she could see that Abilath had no wish to pursue the subject further. There would be other, more favorable times to say what she had in mind to say. Meanwhile they talked and laughed about more congenial matters.

The talk and laughter soon brought Hannah, and while they dressed they told her of their plans to visit a temple.

59

"I do not like it well," Hannah said slowly, "but I cannot see where any harm will be done so long as you remain in your litter outside the gates."

"Can she not enter through the outer portals and wait within the garden?" Abilath coaxed.

"Nay, when you enter, she must draw the curtains and wait in the street outside. Merab will be going to care for you. Leah will go also so that Miriam may not become too weary of waiting."

Abilath wrinkled her nose and set her mouth in a half-pout that made Miriam laugh. "Why must you tease poor Hannah?" she scolded, still laughing. "Rather, let us plan what you will show me."

It was still early in the day when they set out, but already the streets bustled with traffic. There were traders carrying their packs on their backs or driving pack animals, and servants hurrying to the markets to purchase the first and the best of the day's goods.

The morning was clear, with a trace of coolness. Abilath and Miriam settled back in the cushions of their litter. Leah and Merab, mounted on tiny gray donkeys, followed them, with Pash riding a larger white one. There were also two armed men to open the way for them and to see that no one molested them.

"We make quite a caravan!" Miriam exclaimed.

Abilath shrugged. "No, we are insignificantly small. The people we pass will think us to be women of a poor household that can afford no more than one litter and two armed men. You should behold the sight of the cortege when the Old One and the women of Nebuzaradan set out! That is indeed a sight to behold! There are six litters and many armed men and slaves." She sighed deeply. "Someday, after the gods have driven out the evil spirits that bind

60

my leg, I shall marry. Then I, too, will ride to the temple in such a cortege."

Miriam looked about her in wonder as they made their way down streets bordered with trees and gardens. It seemed impossible that this great and beautiful city of abundance could rise out of the desert through which they had journeyed to reach it. They rode past many palaces, where the favorites of Nebuchadnezzar's court lived, and through the cooling shade of groves of trees.

After a time they left the groves and the gardens behind and entered the area of the markets. They passed many open shops where craftsmen worked. They stopped before one of the shops. Miriam glanced out, wondering what god ruled here.

Abilath watched her for a time before saying, "Pash will make some purchases for me here. It would be most unwise for me to visit my gods without the proper gifts."

They moved slowly on through a section of open stalls and into the southern portion of the city. "We near the temple of Enurta," Abilath explained. "His temple is not so large nor so beautiful as Bel Marduk's, for he is not so powerful. Yet, I will stop, for I would not offend him."

Pash came and lifted Abilath from the litter. When they had gone, Leah rode close to where Miriam sat waiting. "Did you ever dream that there was in all the earth a city like unto this one?" she asked excitedly. "Never in all our journeying saw we one to compare!"

"It is even as Eden must have been," Miriam agreed. "Think you that Jerusalem is like this?"

"Nay, I have spoken to one of the servants who has been there. He is also a Judean and loves our city well, but he says that it is not so fair a city to look upon."

Miriam sat for a time in thought, then said, "Yet, Jerusalem is the city of the Most High. Was it not there that He chose to have His temple built?"

Leah frowned. "The man was sad and tearful; perhaps he has forgotten."

When Abilath returned from the temple of Enurta, they moved on to visit the temples of several other gods. They crossed the road that led to the river and the great bridge. Miriam was beginning to feel restless when Abilath announced, "The temple of Bel Marduk comes soon. It is the largest and the most beautiful in the city."

Miriam soon found that what Abilath had said was true. The temple stretched wide and rose high above the street. It was not made of the crude sun-baked bricks, as were so many of the others, but from oven-baked bricks that were glazed and decorated with enamel. A raised design picturing bulls and dragons, sacred to Marduk, ran in a wide frieze that encircled the edifice.

"We are now on the street of Aiburshabu," Abilath explained as Pash placed her back into the litter. "It is down this street that our victorious armies march when they return from battle. The great procession of the Festival of Ishtar passes this way, too."

Ahead loomed a great wall. Miriam had noticed it from the distance and had wondered at the gleaming golden tower that rose high above it, seeming almost to reach to the heavens.

"This is E-temen-an-ki," Abilath explained. "The golden sanctuary is for the god Bel Marduk. See how the sun glints against it! If only Hannah and your Jehovah were not so stubborn, we could enter and you could look upon the great golden form of Bel Marduk. You could see also how his tower rises in great steps that lead up into the very heavens."

As they slowly climbed the arching incline of the wide avenue, Abilath moodily pondered Hannah's restrictions and

Miriam's punctilious obedience to them. The road was smooth as a floor, for it was paved with wide bricks. It was edged with a low protective wall made of many colored pieces of jagged rock cemented together.

They passed the palace of Nebuchadnezzar on the left and two temples of sun-dried brick on the right. "Here I must enter also," Abilath remarked, motioning to the temples. "The second is the temple of our mother goddess, Ishtar. But we will first visit the gardens and rest."

Miriam gasped in wonder at the sight that now spread out before her. On one side of the street there was a wide canal, and on the other side, surrounded by wide lawns, rose a structure so strange and beautiful that she found it hard to believe that she was not dreaming. Huge stone archways rising upward supported wide terraces, from which, in turn, rose other archways that supported higher terraces, and so on up and up. But most astonishing of all were the groves of trees and the gardens of flowers that grew on the terraces, reaching high into the sky. "I must remember," Miriam thought. "I must remember everything about it, so that I can tell my father and Asahel — although they will not believe me."

A smile of proud satisfaction played over Abilath's face as she watched Miriam's unfeigned wonder.

"What is it?" Miriam asked in a hushed voice.

"It is a mountain. Nebuchadnezzar had it made for his Median queen. She was lonely for the mountains of her homeland, so her husband provided one for her. Tell me, do real mountains look like this one?"

Miriam studied the manmade mountain and shook her head slowly. "True, mountains rise upward, but they are mighty in their reach. Some of them are stony, some are wooded. Nay, I never have seen one like this."

Abilath was pleased. "Most people say that it is a fine

reproduction. Come, we will cross over and rest in its coolness."

"But I may not enter!"

"Why not?"

"Did we not agree that I would enter no temples?"

"Come, and do not fear, for this is no temple," Abilath assured her. "We will rest here and be fed and send a gift to the favorite of Nebuchadnezzar. From what I have heard, her favor can do more for a person than the favor of all the gods of Babylon."

Miriam looked at her friend in horror. How did Abilath dare to speak of her gods in such a way? Did she not fear that they would strike her dead? Then she sighed and relaxed. Of course, Abilath's gods could neither help nor harm her. Poor Abilath! She worshiped chunks of stone, for there was only one god, and His name was Jehovah.

While the armed men and the bearers waited, Pash, Abilath, Miriam, and the maidservants crossed the bridge that spanned the canal. They walked across the wide lawn to the stairway. At the foot of the stairway stood two great stone lions, such as Miriam had seen in many places throughout Babylon — for they were sacred to the mother goddess Ishtar.

They stopped on the first terrace and passed through one of the large archways into a shaded area. Pash laid Abilath on one of the richly covered couches with which the room was furnished. "Is it not cool here, even as I promised?" Abilath sighed as she settled back.

Miriam, mute with wonder, stood in the arched entrance, looking out across the lush garden of the terrace to the street below. When she did not answer, Abilath said, "I thought that you would like it here. I hoped that you would find it like your own country, even as the Median does."

"Oh, but I do like it," Miriam turned away from the scene outside and went to sit on the edge of Abilath's couch. "It is so immense and wonderful that I can find no words to match it."

Abilath was amused and gratified at Miriam's amazement. Ringing a tiny gong, she summoned a huge black servant wearing rich robes and many jewels. The slave entered and bowed low before her. Abilath motioned Merab to step closer and said to the servant, "Abilath, of the household of Nebuzaradan, would send a gift to the queen."

The servant bowed again and took the box which Merab held out to him.

He had scarcely gone when another servant entered with fruit and mugs of wine. But before they could begin their lunch, the great black servant returned. "My lady, the Queen of Babylon, would look upon you," he said.

Abilath looked up with a startled frown. "What shall I do? I have dismissed my servant and I cannot walk."

The servant silently stooped and picked her up, motioning for Miriam to follow.

The queen was alone, except for a servant who waved a huge fan of peacock feathers above her head. She watched through narrowed eyes. As they entered, Miriam knew a moment of fear, for the woman did not seem to be in a pleasant mood.

Miriam put an arm about Abilath's waist as the slave gently helped her to stand. Then they both knelt down, bowing their heads to the floor.

"What a lovely child you are," the queen said, looking closely at Abilath. "Never were we told that so rare a flower bloomed in the gardens of Nebuzaradan."

Abilath trembled as Miriam assisted her to rise. "Thank you, my lady. I seldom venture out, because . . ."

"You cannot walk," the queen finished, nodding sympathetically. "We had heard that Nebuzaradan had a niece who was so afflicted. But we must not let it deprive us of your sweet company in the future. You will sit with us at the Festival of Ishtar."

"I am not yet of that age, gracious lady," Abilath said, forgetting that this woman before her was the queen of Babylon, whose slightest wish was law and never to be questioned. Greatly flustered by the error she had made, she flushed and added, "Oh, my lady, who would look on one who is as crippled as I?"

The queen smiled. "You are a most refreshing child. Already you have brightened our dull day. If I could again possess such beauty and youth as are yours, I would not question the gods. However, as you have said, you are too young this year, but there will be other festivals when you are not so young. Then we shall see."

"My gracious lady is wise and most kind," Abilath said, as she bowed again.

The queen turned her eyes to Miriam. She looked at her in silence for a time. "Rumors have reached us of a Judean guest in the house of Nebuzaradan." Then turning to Miriam, she asked her, "What think you of Babylon?"

"In all the world there is none to compare with what I have seen this day," Miriam answered quietly.

"Ah, then you have seen all of the world?" the queen asked. She smiled at the quick flush that rose to Miriam's cheeks.

"Oh, no, most gracious lady, I have seen only a small part of it. But, were there anything more splendid, I would not be able to look upon it."

"Can this compare with the sight of the sun rising out of the wooded hills of my homeland?" the queen asked, waving her hand to include the entire city.

"I have not seen your mountains, gracious lady," Miriam

66

answered, her eyes lowered. She spoke slowly, choosing her words carefully, for she feared that the queen was making fun of her. "My people are told that Jehovah made the heavens and the earth and all that is in them. Even as His power is greater than man's, so must His handiwork be more beautiful."

The queen laughed and clapped her hands with pleasure. "You delight me, child. Now tell me how you first met with Nebuzaradan."

Miriam and Abilath answered her many questions concerning themselves. "I must let you go now," she said at last, "or your servants will become alarmed. But I would see you both again, for I enjoy your visit."

The servant returned to carry Abilath away. The queen frowned as she watched. She said, "I will send my physician to see you. He is in possession of many secrets. Do as he tells you and, perhaps, he can make you walk."

ELEVEN

There was great rejoicing in the households of Babylon. A messenger from Nebuchadnezzar had arrived at the gate of the city an hour before sundown, announcing the approach of the king.

The king was coming and with him would be men from many households. So it was that the season of the Festival of Ishtar came upon them.

The lights burned late in the house of Nebuzaradan, but neither Nebuzaradan nor Urusar came. It was not until the following morning that a messenger from the palace arrived carrying two scrolls — one for the women of Nebuzaradan, and one for Abilath. The household scribe was called to the halls of the women to read the scroll to them.

The sun had climbed nearly to its zenith when the Old One, accompanied by Samilah and the scribe, crossed the garden to Abilath's room, where the scribe was just breaking the seal on Abilath's scroll. At that moment Yaama was escorted into the room. Abilath puckered her nose in distaste. "Why must she come now?" she whispered loudly to Miriam. "Could she not wait, that we might hear our message privately?"

Yaama, bowing low before the Old One, heard and flushed. "Forgive me, but I was overeager to know. . . . Did Urusar return in the night?"

"Nay," the grandmother answered, flashing Abilath a silencing glance. "We are even now waiting to hear the message he has sent us."

"May I stay?" Yaama asked eagerly. She did not wait for an answer but seated herself upon a couch near Samilah. "Perhaps he has enclosed a message for me also."

"You may stay," the dowager replied, "but it is hardly likely that there will be a message for you here. If Urusar has a message for you, it will have been delivered to your father's house."

Yaama flushed at the rebuke but made no move to leave when the scribe unrolled the papyrus and began to read: "To Abilath, the sweet sister of Urusar, greetings!

"I have withstood much teasing this day, for paying the price of a sheet and stylus to send you this message. It seems that no other man has a sister, only a sweetheart.

"Nebuzaradan and I, your brother, wish you to know that we think of you often and pray the gods that they will make you well and strong again.

"There is a great impatience among the men to be about

68

the work of subduing Jerusalem, so that we may return home. At present we but guard the roads, that no food may enter at the gates, while Nebuchadnezzar, in his wisdom, first subdues Lachish.

"Once the battering rams begin their pounding, the city will fall and we will be home with you.

"Greet our little sweetheart, Miriam, and tell her that when it is all over I will search out her handsome Asahel and bring him safely to her.

"Greet for me, also, our adored Old One and the other women of the household — the wise and good Hannah and all of the servants of my uncle's house."

The scribe looked up. "It is sealed with the seal of Urusar."

"Is that all?" Yaama asked.

"It is all," the scribe answered. He rerolled the scroll and handed it back to Abilath.

The Old One sighed. "It will be good to have them home again. Surely there are not too many more nations to conquer."

"At least there will be no more unrest in Judah!" Yaama declared, looking haughtily toward Miriam. "Such scum! It is good to know that we will soon have utterly destroyed their nation!"

"They both write cheerfully," Samilah remarked, ignoring Yaama's rude outburst. "But I fear it may be much longer than we think before we can welcome them home to stay."

Yaama shrugged. "Certainly Nebuzaradan does not think so, for is he not already sending home his plunder?" Miriam winced at Yaama's hinted meaning.

The Old One looked at Miriam and her laughter rang through the room. "Precious plunder she would be! Ah, if she only were, for it is our great loss that she is not.

No, Yaama, Miriam but gives us the pleasure of her sweet company for a little time. Nebuzaradan gives her the love and protection of a daughter of the house."

The color drained from Yaama's face. The Old One had spoken kindly, but Yaama had not missed the warning that they would tolerate no more insults to their guest.

Samilah and the Old One exchanged meaningful glances as Samilah, changing the subject, turned to Yaama and asked, "You are old enough this year to be among those maidens who will be honored at the Festival of Ishtar, are you not?"

"I am old enough," Yaama answered stiffly "but what good will it do me when all of the marriageable young men are away at the wars?"

"Certainly there are some who rode back with Nebuchadnezzar, and there are the scribes and the scholars," Samilah reminded her.

"They do not interest me." She rose to her feet and looked around uncertainly. "I must return to my home. Perhaps there was a message left there for me. Someone must have forgotten to deliver it."

Miriam's eyes were full of pity as she watched Yaama cross the room to the door. She thought, "Now I understand why she hates me. It is because I am Urusar's friend."

When she had gone, the Old One said, "It is not good when a young lady lays bare her heart for all to see."

"I will send a message to Urusar and tell him that next time he must send her a message, too," Abilath decided. "Surely, if he knew how happy it would make her . . ."

"No, no, it would not do at all, my child," the Old One interrupted. "When you have become as old as I, you will know that each heart must earn its own happiness. It is not something that can be given by another." She sighed and affectionately stroked Miriam's hair. "Happiness must come from within. Our Miriam has it and I think you are finding it, my child."

The return of Nebuchadnezzar set off a season of revelry, in the streets and the temples of Babylon, that would end in the Festival of Ishtar. It was Ishtar, goddess of love and nature, who, they believed, gave them bountiful harvests. So it was that each spring, at planting time, they held a lavish festival in her honor, in order that she might be pleased with them and watch over their fields.

The din of the throngs in the street of Aiburshabu filled Nebuzaradan's house also. As the day of the festival drew near, the wives and the Old One made their plans. Even the servants would attend, joining the throngs that eddied through the streets.

"Only I, of all Babylon, must stay like a caged bird within my own garden," Abilath fretted.

"Do not weep," Miriam soothed her, "only believe that another year will find you with the others on the terraces of the Median's gardens. Your walking improves daily. Certainly with the help of the queen's own physician and the prayers I offer daily to Jehovah, we cannot fail to make you walk."

Abilath nodded and Miriam could see her determination hardening.

Although Miriam wondered about the Festival of Ishtar, there was another day coming soon about which she did not need to ask. It was the Passover, the feast of the unleavened bread. "We will eat the Paschal feast at the house of my brother in Kifil," Hannah had told her when she first arrived in Babylon.

Miriam was excited as the day drew near. It would be her first visit to the village that stood on the banks of the

Chebar. Leah had visited there often with Hannah, but Miriam had not wanted to leave Abilath alone. However, since she was now somewhat improved, Miriam felt free to leave her friend for a few days.

Abilath watched her as she dressed, her mouth drooping in sadness. "I wish that I were going with you," she said.

Miriam paused in her preparations to put her arms around her friend in a tight hug. "You will scarcely miss me. What fun it will be for you to spend the night in the hall of the women. I hear that much has been planned for your entertainment."

"We must hurry," Hannah cautioned as they made their way across the courtyard. "If we do not, we shall not reach my brother's house before sundown."

Three donkeys waited for them at the gate, and with them was Eli, son of Hannah's brother Ephram. Miriam studied him carefully from the corner of her eyes. This was the young man who, the day after Passover, would be betrothed to Leah. She was pleased by his appearance and a little puzzled. When her father had spoken of the people in bondage, she had pictured them as downtrodden and suffering from want. This young man walked proudly, and his tunic was of fine-textured material that hinted of wealth.

Upon their arrival, Miriam almost immediately felt at home. The house of Ephram was a spacious house, built of sun-dried brick. There was little here to remind one of Babylon. It was a piece of Judah transplanted to the banks of the Chebar.

Servants came and led them to their rooms, and all of the time Miriam looked curiously about her. She thought, "I must tell my father of this house and the people whom I meet here." There was none of the rich splendor here that she had found in the house of Nebuzaradan, but she could not question that it was the house of a rich man. She wondered about the man Ephram. To a servant she said, "This is my first visit to Kifil."

"I know. We all hope that you will be comfortable here," the girl answered shyly.

"Oh, yes! It is a lovely house, one like my father's house. I had not thought to find such a house in Kifil."

The girl smiled proudly. "My master is a ruler among his people and chief steward at the great house of Sarsechim, prince of Babylon. His son Eli has long trained under him and even at so young an age he is already second only to his father." She paused and flushed uneasily. "Forgive me, my lady, I would not bore you."

"I find these things very interesting," Miriam assured her.

Hannah came with Leah and the three of them went to join the other women. They would all go in to the feast as soon as Ephram had finished the ritual of searching his house, to be certain that no leavening remained.

A woman rose and came to greet them. "My sister, welcome to the house of Ephram!" She embraced Hannah and turned to lay an arm about Leah's waist. "Leah, my dear, it is good to have you with us this day."

Hannah took Miriam's hand and drew her into the circle. "This is Talaria, of whom you have heard me speak."

"May the Lord Jehovah bless the lady Talaria and her household," Miriam said, bowing.

Talaria smiled. "Welcome to this house, Miriam, daughter of Simeon. I have heard much concerning you."

Miriam was surprised to find such a large group of people gathered under a single roof for the Paschal feast. She wondered how many rooms and how many lambs would be needed, for by the law no less than ten or more than twenty

73

could eat at one table. Even after the guests had been divided into groups, there was a goodly number who sat at the family table. Miriam found herself placed between Hannah and Talaria. Leah was at the other side of the table, with Eli beside her. They were speaking softly together. Leah flushed with pleasure.

Hannah leaned near to Miriam and said softly, "He is pleased with her."

Miriam smiled. It was easy to see that Leah was pleased also. Miriam was glad. It would be hard for her to leave Leah behind when she returned to Judah, but not too hard, now that she knew Leah would be happy here.

It was difficult for Miriam to keep her mind on the long ritual which preceded the feast. Her mind was filled with memories of her parents and home. Her throat ached with her desire to be in her homeland. When they passed the cup of wine, she could scarcely swallow because of the lump that was in her throat. She blinked hard to keep back the tears of homesickness that burned her eyelids.

Talaria reached out and took her hand. "On such a night it is always hard to be away from those we love," she said sympathetically.

Miriam nodded slightly and swallowed hard.

"Will there be many relatives gathered beneath your father's roof at home in Judah?"

"Only a few," Miriam answered. "And the household of Caleb is always there. My father had no sons. Asahel, son of Caleb, always takes the place of the son of the house." She flushed, embarrassed that she had spoken so freely of her family, but just being able to talk about them had eased her homesickness.

"I cannot know who will be there this year. Asahel is a scribe at the court of Jerusalem. It is not likely, if the

74

city is in siege, that he will be able to join them." She paused, remembering Urusar's letter. What was the fate of the city? "But it might still be possible . . ."

"Yes," Talaria said soothingly, "nothing is impossible."

Their friendly talk was interrupted by the men, who were arguing rather loudly. Miriam turned to listen.

"It is inconceivable that Jehovah would again choose to enslave His people," a flushed young man exclaimed.

Miriam smiled and thought, "It is just what Asahel might be saying."

"Aye," another agreed, "perhaps you are right. I pray that you are."

"I know that I am right!"

"But, should Jerusalem fall, would you join those who flee to Egypt?" the other asked.

The young man shrugged. "I know not. I like not the yoke of bondage. If Jerusalem falls, what matter where we are?"

Ephram nodded thoughtfully and mused, "One hears of great wickedness in the court of Zedekiah. It is said that he listens not to the counseling of Jeremiah."

"And who is this man Jeremiah?" the young man demanded. "There are many who call him a traitor! How can we know that he is truly a prophet sent by Jehovah?"

"Nay, he must not say such things!" Miriam objected.

Talaria turned to her and asked, "You know this man Jeremiah?"

"Yes, and he is a goodly man. Often he has visited in my father's house."

Ephram looked thoughtfully at the young man, then said, "Only today I heard rumors that the armies of Egypt are marching to deliver Jerusalem. Yet, it was only a rumor. If only we could know what is really happening!"

"And if this be true, it will prove that Jeremiah is not a true prophet of Jehovah!" the young man interrupted excitedly.

"Only rumors," Hannah remarked to Talaria. "We hear so many rumors."

"Even at home, near as we were to Jerusalem, we knew little more," Miriam assured her. "Even Asahel, on his visits from the city itself, would always say, 'It is so rumored.'"

Realizing that it was time to conclude the supper, Ephram interrupted the conversation and requested all present to sing a psalm. Then he spoke a familiar benediction.

As they rose to leave, Ephram announced to the men, "Come, we will talk more of these things. I have a guest arriving soon who may be able to answer your questions."

After the women had retired, the men awaited the arrival of the guest, and while they waited, they filled the time with lively talk.

The first rays of day had scarcely tinged the eastern sky when Miriam awoke to find Hannah bending over her. "Arise quickly and dress yourself," Hannah instructed her. "There is one outside in the garden who would speak with you."

It seemed to Miriam that she would never finish dressing, even with Hannah's help. Her hands trembled and her fingers were sticks, refusing to do her bidding. "Who is it?" she whispered.

Hannah shook her head. "I know not. A servant came to me and said only that one well known to your father wishes to speak with you."

Miriam hurried down the long hallway and out through an arched doorway to a stairway that led to the garden below. She was halfway down the stairs when she saw him. Even in the half-light, she could not be mistaken. "Asahel!"

76

she exclaimed as she ran to meet him. "Oh, Asahel, how came you to find me here?" she sobbed. "It is good that you have come to take me home, for I almost feared that my father had forgotten me."

"This is no time for tears! I have only a few minutes to spend with you. Would you have me tell your father that I came and found you weeping?"

"Tell me of my father and my mother. Are they both well?" she asked, wiping her eyes.

"They are well, but there has been much sickness and some deaths." He paused, looking down at her sadly, then added, "My father's and Deborah's among them."

Deborah and Caleb both dead! Miriam found it hard to believe. Surely it could not be the ones she had known and loved.

"Sickness broke out in Jerusalem," Asahel was explaining, "and was spread throughout the countryside by the deserters who escaped over the walls at night."

"And you?" Miriam asked. A sudden fear had gripped her heart. "Have you also deserted?"

"Nay, I am even now on a mission for Zedekiah. He sent me secretly to visit the leaders of this village. They do not know my name and they must not. That is why I could not go directly to Ephram and ask permission to see you."

Miriam nodded and looked up at him questioningly. He was telling her that she had been mistaken in his mission. He had not, then, come after her.

"Saw you the young man Eli?" she asked, to cover her disappointment.

"Aye, it is he whom I must thank for these few minutes with you. He could think and talk of nothing but his lovely Leah. So it was that I found out that you, too, were in this house."

"She is very happy with Hannah's choice."

Asahel laughed softly. "And well she may be. I do not doubt that Leah's father will be pleased also."

"You are changed," he said slowly after silently observing Miriam for some time. "It is almost as though I did not know you. But I cannot say that I do not like the change, for I do. You seemed but a child when you left us." He paused and shook his head, as though he were trying to shake off some dream. Then he sobered. "I wish it were my good fortune to be the one sent by your father to return you to his house. You tempt me, for I would like to know this lovely lady you have become."

"I would go with you," she said shyly.

"Nay, that is not possible, but I pray that your father may send for you soon."

There was a woman's call from beyond the garden. Asahel affectionately embraced her for a moment, and was gone. Miriam stood where he had left her, listening for some sound of his leaving, but she heard nothing. She wondered about the strange joy she had felt in his presence and the sharp sorrow at his parting. He had said that she was changed, and truly she must be, for she had never felt this way before.

Hannah came and put an arm around her shoulders. "Come, my dear. It would never do for anyone to find you here in the garden at this early hour."

They went back to her room, and Hannah persuaded her to go back to bed again. "Your Asahel is a handsome young man," she said quietly, "and one of whom you may well be proud."

Miriam looked up in surprise. "No one was to know his name! How could you know?"

"It was not hard to know, not when I saw you together. Do not fear for his safety, for I will not tell."

TWELVE

The seasons passed, and it was already over a year since Miriam had first entered the house of Nebuzaradan. Each day she waited for the messenger who would come from her father with word that she should return. But no messenger came. "My father has forgotten me here," she would whisper to Leah.

"Nay," Leah would answer, "only be patient."

Word had been received of the fall of the city of Lachish, and there was much rejoicing in the streets of Babylon, but there was no rejoicing in the households of Kifil. Nor had they rejoiced at the rumors that the Egyptian army had turned back before it even reached the borders of Judah.

Miriam listened and wondered. She would have been more saddened by the news, and more worried by the delay in her father's plans, if she had not been so interested in the progress that Abilath was making. They exercised the leg every day, as the queen's physician had ordered, and Merab massaged the muscles to loosen them. After a long series of such treatments, Abilath was able, with only occasional assistance, to walk to her couch in the garden or to other parts of the estate.

"It is a miracle!" Samilah exclaimed, hugging Abilath close, as the three of them walked to the women's quarters one day.

"There is still a limp." Abilath frowned.

"But it grows less every day," Samilah insisted.

A few days later, Samilah accompanied Miriam and

Abilath as far as the garden gate after they had visited the women's quarters.

Having entered their own room, Abilath rolled over on her couch so that Merab could rub and knead her leg with the ointments which the queen's physician had provided.

Hannah burst breathless into the room. "We hear good news!" she exclaimed. "Word has just reached us that Nebuchadnezzar nears the city!"

Abilath swung quickly around and into a sitting position, nearly upsetting Merab and the tray of ointments. "Will Urusar be with him?" Then she paused, frowning. "You are certain that it is not just another rumor?"

"Yes, I am certain," Hannah replied, laughing at Abilath's frown. "I know not about Urusar, but the news was given to us by a peddler who was at the gate when the king's messenger arrived."

Abilath lay back and motioned for Merab to continue with the treatment. She turned her head on her arms, so that she faced Miriam, to ask her, "Think you that he will be pleased with my walking?"

"He will be pleased, and your uncle also."

"My uncle will not be coming. He can never return until the campaign is over."

As Miriam was playing her harp and singing for Abilath, Urusar entered the room. He had already been in the house for many hours, but no one had told them of his arrival. "Urusar!" Abilath cried as she walked toward him.

"Look! What is this?" he exclaimed, lifting her high in his embrace. "My little sister, you walk! And no one told me!"

"It was to be a surprise." She stood back so that he might see her better.

"It is indeed a surprise," he said, hugging her close again.

80

Miriam had stopped her playing when he entered and sat happily watching. Now he turned and, pointing to her, asked, "Are you not going to introduce me to your friend?"

Abilath laughed. "Stop your teasing. You know quite well who that is."

"No! It cannot be our little Miriam!" He shook his head, as though in wonder.

Miriam smiled sweetly and strummed a fading chord on her harp. "We may have changed, Abilath, but your brother has not."

Urusar laughed at them. "Truly, now I know that it is Miriam. Do you know, my sweet sister, once she actually told me that there was another man more handsome than I — and it turned out to be old Anak." He walked around the room in an imitation of the old man's bent back and bowed legs. "Maybe my heart is not so good as his, but of a certainty, I must insist, I am the more handsome!"

When Miriam could stop laughing, she denied, "It is not true!"

"Ah, no, now I remember," he mused, with a sly wink at Abilath. "It was some stranger named Asahel. I think she could scarcely remember him."

Miriam blushed, in spite of a determined effort not to. "You are both handsome," she insisted.

The days that followed were exciting days for the two girls. Urusar's unexpected visits and his entertaining accounts of his experiences amused them and gave them much to talk about when he was gone.

It was on the second day that he turned to Abilath and said, "Today I was with Kingal, the brother of your friend Yaama." He paused and chuckled. "He told me to remind you that once, when you were both very young, he promised that you would be his first and favorite wife."

"It was long ago," Abilath answered with a shrug. "If he is like his sister, he will not be easily pleased with the likes of me."

Urusar pulled a long face. "Are you not interested in what else he had to say?"

Miriam smiled. "Do not urge him, Abilath, or I fear that he will build it to so great a story that we will never know what was truly said."

"For that, I have half a mind to tell you nothing!" he countered in mock outrage.

"Oh, come, my brother," Abilath soothed, "I am breathless to hear."

"We made a plan," he began, unable to keep his secret longer, "one that we hope you will both find pleasing. Tomorrow is festival day and we would like to show you both the sights of the day."

Miriam turned to Hannah. "Oh, Hannah, may we?"

"I see no reason why Abilath may not go," Hannah said thoughtfully. "But for you — I do not know what to say. . . . With you it is different. I fear your father would not like to know that you attended the festival of a false goddess."

"Fear not, Hannah, we will respect your wishes and enter into no temple," Urusar promised. "We would only show her the parades and the streets filled with people."

Hannah sighed deeply. "I know not what to say, except that I find it not to my liking."

"Say yes, Hannah, please say yes," Abilath coaxed. "I would like to go, but I cannot bear to leave her here alone."

"Do you wish to go?" Hannah asked Miriam.

"Oh, yes!" Miriam answered. She paused, looking down at her hands, trying not to let anyone know how badly she wanted to go. "Yet I would not offend Jehovah."

"How can I say no?" Hannah said, after a few moments

82

more of thought. "I trust Urusar to look to your safety. Only, you must promise that you will enter no temple."

When Urusar was gone, Abilath threw her arms around Miriam in a tight hug. "Oh, Miriam, it is to be even as you once said! This year I shall attend the festival."

"Will we sit with the women of Nebuzaradan?"

Abilath frowned thoughtfully. "I do not know."

"Ah, and what is it that you do not know?" someone interrupted.

The two girls turned, startled by the voice. Yaama stood smiling at them from the doorway.

"How did you get in here?" Abilath demanded with obvious irritation.

Yaama shrugged and crossed the room to join them. "I saw no reason to wait for Merab to bring me. After all, I know the way."

"What is it that you want?" Abilath asked bluntly, watching her through narrowed eyes.

"Must I always want something when I come to see you?" Yaama challenged. "It is only that I seek the quiet of your house. The din of the revelers on the street of Aiburshabu echoes through my father's house and gardens until one can scarcely stand it."

"It must be interesting and exciting. Can you watch the people from your window?"

"Who would care to?" she shrugged. "It is but the rabble. I could not even have come today if Saris had not agreed to accompany me. It takes all of my father's armed men to protect the gates of the house so that the revelers do not enter it and plunder."

"Saris? Of what family is he?" Abilath asked, with quick interest.

"He is only one of the guards from the garrison. He finds me attractive, and there is nothing that he would not do for me. I find him very useful at times like this. If you like, you may see him in the entrance court below."

The three girls walked a little too eagerly down the hall to the lattice, where they could look down to the court below. "He is old!" Miriam whispered in surprise.

"I did not say that he pleased me, only that I found him useful."

Abilath wrinkled her nose in distaste and remarked, "I do not like him. You may have your Saris to guard you, but I would not have him around. He would frighten me, and I would not trust one so cruel-looking."

"Indeed, he does have the look of a cruel man. I would also fear him," Miriam agreed.

Yaama laughed. "I doubt not that he is as cruel as he looks. Is he not a soldier? A man must have some streak of cruelty in him to be a soldier, do you not agree?"

"No!" Abilath objected angrily. "Certainly you do not think my uncle a cruel man — or Urusar."

Could Yaama be right, Miriam wondered. She thought of Urusar and Nebuzaradan, trying to picture each in battle. Asahel was now a soldier too. Was there a core of hardness in Asahel also?

"All men are cruel! Has not Urusar been home for three days without so much as sending me a message?" Yaama complained.

"It is little enough that any of us see him." Abilath answered lightly. "There are many things he must do and many friends that he would like to visit."

"And I am not one of those friends? Tell me, Abilath, do you think Urusar likes me?"

"Why do you ask such a question of me?"

"I would like to know whether he has mentioned me."

Abilath frowned impatiently. "I do not remember, although he did say that he had seen your brother Kingal."

84

"Would Urusar come to your garden if you asked?" Yaama continued.

Abilath clamped her lips in irritation. "I do not know. Have you no pride that you will let him know how much you want to see him? If you wait, he will surely come to you."

Miriam was silent as she listened to them. She had never liked Yaama, but now she could not help feeling sorry for her.

"What good will it do me to wait if he does not come?" Yaama demanded. "Is he home now?"

"I do not know." Abilath answered.

"So you do not know!" Yaama mimicked angrily. "Why do you not send Miriam to find out?"

"Have you forgotten that Miriam is a guest in this house and not a servant?" Abilath reminded her.

"I care not whom you send, but send someone."

"You have no right to come here ordering me about!" Abilath asserted angrily. "If you would send someone to summon him, then go back to your own house and send one of your own servants. Merab is busy, too."

Miriam smiled, although she felt uncomfortable. Their fighting seemed quite useless. "Why do you quarrel over this?" she asked.

They turned, and momentarily it seemed as though they would both pounce upon her when, quietly, she added, "I will find Leah and she may carry your message. Surely, if Urusar is not busy, he will welcome a summons to join you."

"Miriam speaks wisely." Yaama smiled triumphantly at Abilath.

For a moment Miriam was afraid that Abilath was going to be very angry. Then she smiled. "Do as you will," she said.

Leah was nowhere to be found, so Miriam went to search

for Urusar. She could hear his voice even before she entered the lower hall. He was arguing. She was tempted to turn back. Then she heard the quieting voice of the household scribe and hurried on. Urusar looked up as she entered. "Now this is a pleasure I had not expected!" he exclaimed, seeming to forget his recent anger.

"I but run an errand. Yaama is with Abilath. She wishes to see you."

"I spoke too soon. You may tell her that I have been called away on business for the king."

Miriam was not satisfied. "Your excuse is not a good enough reason. She longs to see you and, besides, her many questions are making Abilath angry."

"Why must she always bother me?"

"Have you anything better to do?" Miriam answered.

It did not take long for Miriam to discover that she had not been wise when she urged him to come. He was sullen and unresponsive until Yaama asked, "Would you not like to attend me at the Festival of Ishtar?"

Urusar leaned forward and looked at her intently. "Has no one told you that when a young man desires your company he will seek it?"

Yaama looked at him, unable to believe what she had heard. The color drained from her cheeks, and her angry eyes narrowed down to slits. She asked, "Am I to understand that you do not desire my company?"

"I do not desire your company," was Urusar's defiant answer.

"Then I have been right all along! You prefer the Judean. That is why you brought her here."

"I did not bring her here," he answered quietly; "my uncle did."

"But you do not deny that you prefer her!" Turning to

86

Miriam, she added, "Now I see why you were so willing to bring him. It was so that you might stand smugly by and see me humiliated! You will be sorry for this!" she threatened as she left them in arrogant anger.

When she was gone, Abilath said, "You need not have angered her, Urusar. Already she is cruel to Miriam."

"I am sorry if I have caused trouble, but there are some people who do not understand kindness. I had to be cruel to her to make her understand."

THIRTEEN

Miriam paused to let a shouting group of revelers pass. She drew back, so that they would not brush against her gown, but she felt soiled by having been so near to them.

"Do not be offended by them," Urusar said, laughing. "They have but taken too much free wine on their way to the temple."

"Is it part of their worship?" she asked. It was not worship as she had learned to know it in her father's house. Such loud, coarse laughter would have been regarded as blasphemous at the altar of Jehovah.

Urusar drew her along to a point where the flagstones of the Aiburshabu road gave way to one of the many parks of Babylon. They found a shaded bench and sat down to wait for Abilath and Yaama's brother Kingal to catch up. Miriam watched the passing people. "Never have I seen so many people," she remarked to Urusar.

He smiled and said, "And they are from many nations. The group yonder are Medes, and the man who follows is from Edom."

Miriam turned and watched them disappear into the crowd. "How can you tell from where they come?" she asked.

"It is not hard, once you learn to distinguish their features and their robes. The bones of their faces differ, also the slant of their eyes and the color of their hair and skin," he explained.

A group of dancers was performing a short distance away. Miriam looked at the performance for a minute or two. She felt strangely excited and, at the same time, she blushed at the wild movements of their half-naked bodies. Hannah had been right, she thought guiltily. This was no place for a daughter of Judah. She turned her back on the dancers and again observed the people walking about in the park.

When Abilath and Kingal came, the four of them moved slowly on. They paused to listen to a band playing beside the road. "It nears the time for the parade to start," Kingal reminded them. "Would it not be wise for us to find a place from which we can watch?"

"Yes, a place where we can sit and watch," Urusar amended. "We must not allow Abilath to become overtired, or Hannah will scold."

"Let us go a little farther down the Aiburshabu," Kingal suggested. "The greater crowds will try to stay close to the temple and follow after the parade to E-temen-an-ki, the tower of Marduk."

"Wisely spoken, my friend," Urusar agreed.

They moved on through the crowd. Most of the people, as Kingal had predicted, were going in the opposite direction.

They had not long to wait before Nebuchadnezzar, in all his kingly splendor, rode past with his retinue of princes in chariots. Behind them followed the priests. Miriam watched with wide eyes, scarcely believing that the world could hold such splendor.

Abilath leaned close and whispered, "The priestesses are coming. Always I have heard the women talk of their great beauty and exclaim over the elegance of their attire."

Urusar was amused at ther interest. "Today you will note well what they wear, so that you may copy it tomorrow. It is the way of women."

Miriam scarcely heard him as she watched the women parading slowly past. Some laughed and waved at the people; others walked with their eyes downcast. There were women of every build and nation, but all were richly gowned in a rainbow of colors and gleaming with jewels.

The crowds surged past them, cutting off their view. "Come," Urusar said. "We must hurry or we will miss the crowning of Zoganes, the clown king." As they walked on, Urusar explained, "Each year at this time, there is such a one crowned for the entertainment of the people. He is usually one already condemned to death, for at the end of his rule he must die."

Miriam shuddered. She had heard that those who worshiped idols often sacrificed people instead of lambs. Could this man be such a sacrifice?

They found a place close to E-temen-an-ki, and Miriam watched with interest as Nebuchadnezzar placed his hands upon the huge golden image of the god.

"The god Marduk is now bestowing strength and wisdom on Nebuchadnezzar, that he may rule us well through the coming year," Kingal explained.

The crowd moved forward, jostling them along. Slowly they worked their way toward the booths and the stalls where food would be supplied. They passed through an area of booths where little idols of the goddess Ishtar were being sold and where the street was filled with the sellers of wine and spiced cakes, meats and cheeses. The air was charged with the odor of food. Miriam felt hunger curling in her stomach. She was glad when Urusar said, "Beyond this are the pavilions where we may eat."

"I would carefully choose the one I entered," Kingal teased, glancing sideways at Urusar. "Else you may meet up with the wrath of my sister."

"Never fear, I will watch," Urusar promised. "I am sorry that I was so harsh with Yaama."

Kingal snorted, "It will do her no harm to find that she cannot always have everything she wants."

The setting sun glinted red against the golden shrine at the top of the tower of Marduk. As they emerged from the dining pavilion, Urusar said, "We must hurry, or it will be dark before we reach my uncle's house. Hannah warned that we must be home early."

"Let Abilath ride," Miriam suggested when they reached the place where they had left the litter. "I would like to walk for a way." She breathed in deeply the cooling breeze that always came at the time of sunset.

After a time she said to Urusar, "You have told me nothing of my land, and how its people fare."

"I would not grieve you," he said softly.

"The fighting goes badly for them?"

Urusar walked in silence for a time before answering. "It is hard to speak of war with softened words, for war is harsh."

"Tell me in harsh words, then, for it is so that I heard of it in my father's house."

"There is great suffering in the city of Jerusalem and all the countryside," he began slowly. "I do not understand

90

how the city has stood so long against us. It was Nebuchadnezzar's plan to starve them into submission. We even
poisoned the water. Yet, enough supplies are smuggled over
the walls each night to sustain life. Even the plague that
rages within the walls has not forced them into submission."

Miriam nodded thoughtfully. "I have heard of the sickness. Deborah contracted it from a deserter and died."

"I did not know," Urusar said softly. He turned and
looked down at her, deep in thought. "When heard you
last from your father's house?"

She paused when she recalled that Asahel had warned
her against telling anyone of his visit, and it was the first
time that she had mentioned anything that he had told
her. "It was but a rumor I heard in Kibil," she said, trying
to be casual.

"You do not lie easily," he said softly. "Who is it that
you seek to protect, Anak or Asahel?"

"It is Asahel," she answered reluctantly, "but it was
a long time ago."

"Then he did not come to my uncle's house?"

"Nay."

"Has he been back since?"

Miriam looked up at Urusar, but she could not read his
thoughts. "I know not," she said. "I would not have seen
him then if he had not learned by chance that I was in the
village."

"He was a fool to take such a chance!" Urusar bent
close to Miriam and whispered, "Tell no one else what you
have told me this night, for Nebuchadnezzar would not be
pleased with the news that a soldier of Zedekiah had visited
some people of Judah in Kifil."

"No one else knows and I am sorry that you do."

"No, little Miriam, it is well that I do." He reached out
and took her hand. "I will make you a promise to prove

my friendship. When we have subdued Jerusalem, I will do my best to bring Asahel to you."

"How can you be so certain that you are going to subdue them?"

Urusar laughed in surprise at the question. "Think you the mouse can defeat the lion in battle?"

"Aye," she answered in quick defense, "if Jehovah fights beside the mouse."

"I hear much of the power of your Jehovah," Urusar answered lightly. "I have even heard rumors that he now advises his people to come to Babylon. Can it not be that he considers his power to be not equal to the power of Nebuchadnezzar?"

Miriam looked up in horror. "Nay, Urusar! Do not question the power of the Most High! It is true that Jeremiah says that Jehovah sends us into exile again, but only to punish us. The people of Judah have turned from Him and He would chastise them to bring them back. But even yet He may relent if Zedekiah but calls Jeremiah to him and heeds his words."

"Do you really believe this, Miriam?" Urusar asked quietly.

"Indeed, I believe that there is only one god and it is Jehovah. If He wills, He can stop the sun or the moon in their passing. He can even strengthen the weak arms of the armies of Judah that they may destroy the might that is Babylon."

"It seems that not all of your people are as certain of these things as you seem to be. I saw many at the Festival of Ishtar this day."

Miriam flushed uncomfortably. "Could they not have come, even as I did, to see the many people and the parade?" she asked hopefully.

92

He shook his head. "Many there are who will enter the temples and give themselves to worship."

"Then it is even as Jeremiah has told us!" she cried, horrified at the thought. "Jehovah has reason to punish His people!"

FOURTEEN

Ten days had passed since the festival of the goddess Ishtar. Nebuchadnezzar was gone and his men with him. The city was slowly settling back into its usual quiet.

Miriam walked restlessly through the garden. The sun was hot, but she could not rest today, as Abilath did. There were too many questions crowding through her mind. For months she had wondered about the charges which Yaama had made. Was she really a guest, or was she a slave within this household? Certainly Urusar had not treated her as a slave. Yet, how could she be certain that his kindness was not part of some agreement made with her father? It was not impossible that he had used her, and Nebuzaradan's affection for her, to insure the safety of the rest of his household, knowing that she would be safe here. All she knew for certain was that her father had not sent for her as he had said he would.

She knew that there were those who could answer her questions, but she was afraid to hear their answers. Would it not be better to ask and know? "As soon as the Old One wakens, I shall seek an audience with her and I will ask," she decided.

Deeply absorbed in her thoughts, Miriam did not notice

that Merab was standing at the garden gate. She was startled when she heard the servant announce, "Hannah would speak with you in the lower hall."

Miriam hurried inside, where Hannah waited. Hannah motioned her into a guest chamber and closed the door behind them. For a moment Miriam stood in stunned silence as she stared at the man who awaited her there. Then she threw her arms about him in a tight embrace. "Anak! Oh, Anak! when did you come?"

"I have only this hour arrived. Even now I am on my way to Kifil with a message I carry."

So he also had come to deliver a message. She blinked away the tears that welled up in her eyes. "Is there a message from my father's house?" she asked.

Anak nodded. "I come that you may return." He frowned, as though there was more that he must tell her, and she asked, "Is something wrong?"

"Your father is not well. We must leave at once, that he may see you once more."

"If he is ill, why did he not send for me?"

"You were safe here. He would not call you back to the hardships that fill our lives."

She turned away so that he would not see her tears. How could she have been so happy, forgetting the hardships of her people?

"Go now and tell Abilath," Hannah said.

Miriam made her way slowly back to Abilath's room. Now that it was time to return to her homeland, she found that her sorrow at leaving was as great as her joy at the thought of seeing her loved ones once more. She had entered the room and closed the door behind her before she realized that Abilath was not alone. Yaama was with her, and at the moment she was upbraiding Abilath, say-

94

ing, "You deliberately let me make a fool of myself, knowing that Urusar planned to show the festival to the daughter of Judah!"

Yaama heard Miriam enter and swung around to face her. "And you! Thought you to make a fool of Yaama, princess of Babylon?"

"Why did you not come while Urusar was here, that he might answer you?" Abilath demanded, but Yaama made no answer as she crossed to where Miriam stood.

"I would not have you think harshly of me when I am gone," Mariam said gently. "And even now I prepare to leave for Judah."

"So, now you would run away! Know you not that Jerusalem may even now be leveled with the ground and that you are part of the spoils of war? You are the property of Babylon, to be disposed of as Nebuchadnezzar sees fit."

"Yaama be still!" Abilath ordered.

Yaama turned and smiled icily at Abilath." You are afraid for her and will try to help her, but it will do no good. I will send Saris to notify my father." As a parting word, she threatened Miriam, "He will know how to treat a runaway slave."

"You are no longer safe beneath this roof," Abilath sobbed, when Yaama was gone. "If she goes to her father, it is not likely that he will listen even to the Old One."

When Hannah came, they told her what had happened. "This is no time for weeping," she scolded.

Miriam looked from one to the other. She felt strangely calm as she decided on a plan. She took off her girdle and gown. "I will dress in Leah's clothing," she said. "If Leah may go for the night, we can go together to Kifil."

"Aye," Hannah agreed. "Go to the house of Ezekiel. There you will find Anak." She wrapped Leah's long, dark cloak about Miriam's shoulders and pulled the hood down to cover her hair. "Jehovah go with you and protect you," she said.

Miriam embraced Abilath in a quick farewell, and the two girls hurried away.

The guards leaned impatiently against the gate. "Hurry, if you would pass through," they yelled. "Is it not enough that we stand here all day? Would you keep us here the night also?"

They passed quickly through the gate and it swung to behind them. But before the chains had been set, a man's voice called, "Hold! I seek a runaway slave. Has one passed this way?"

The two girls stood rooted to the ground, looking wildly about for a place to hide. The gate began to open again. Miriam grasped Leah's arm and drew her back into the shadow of the great gate, where they would be partly hidden.

"Many have passed through this gate," one of the guards snorted. "How would I know which would be running away?"

"Hold your tongue and think well! This slave is of the household of Nebuzaradan," said the other.

The guard spat hard into the dust at his feet. "Think you I spend my time sitting on the back step of Nebuzaradan's house, that I know the faces of his slaves?"

"It might have been better if you had. Remain here, while I go into Kifil to seek her."

The two men walked so close to Miriam that she could have reached out and touched them. She recognized one of them. It was Saris, the garrison guard and willing tool of the treacherous Yaama.

"The lady does not waste time," Leah hinted.

"I have no time to think about Yaama," Miriam answered. "Come, we must hurry."

They did not take the wide road that the men had taken, but rather a path that led through a grove at the river bank. "You are sure that you know the way?" Miriam asked as the shadows of a strange street closed about her.

"Aye," Leah assured her. "At Joseph's shop we will turn onto the street of the weavers."

The deepening shadows had darkened the street until all of the shuttered shops looked much alike. Miriam glanced at Leah. A fear was rising within her, a growing certainty that they had lost their way.

Leah started to cry. Miriam moved closer to comfort her. "The moon will soon rise," she said softly. "Then we will go back over the way we have come. This time we will not miss the street."

"We did not find it in the light; how can we hope to find it in the darkness?" Leah sobbed.

"Hush! Would you arouse the people and set Yaama's guards against us?"

They turned back, but they had only gone a few steps when, not far ahead, a torch appeared. The girls dashed into a dark areaway between two houses. The light drew nearer. One of the men asked, "Think you that the man Ezekiel was lying? We know that the woman was not in his house, but is it not possible that he knows where they hide her?"

"No. More likely they have taken her elsewhere."

"And where might that be?" the first demanded angrily. "Would you search the whole village?"

"Hold your peace and know that, if need be, we will search every house!"

As the unsuspecting guards moved on, the girls remained

in their hiding place till the immediate danger had passed. Then Leah said, "I think now that I know the way, yet I wonder whether it is safe for us to go there. They will return when they do not find us elsewhere."

"If we go quickly, we will be there and gone before they return," Miriam replied.

It was impossible to go quickly through the darkness of the strange street. "We must take care that we do not go too far," Leah whispered.

"Aye," Miriam agreed. The usual fetid odors of the street were intensified by the darkness. The odors, along with her excitement and fear, sickened her.

Then, without warning, a strange sense of danger shot through her. She knew that Leah felt it, too, for there was a tightening of the hand that held hers.

Miriam held her breath and strained to hear some sound which might identify the presence of someone in the darkness. Her first thought was of the scavenger dogs, fierce wild dogs who stole through the streets at night, eating the refuse thrown there. Her spine tingled with a sense of something or someone standing near.

"Fear not, Leah, my dear betrothed; it is I, Eli," a voice whispered out of the darkness.

Miriam took a great gasping breath of relief, as he added, "Here take my hand, we must hurry." Leah took his other hand.

The houses thinned out and Miriam noticed that they were again hurrying through the groves at the river's edge. "Where do you take me?" she asked.

"I was at the house of Ezekiel when the men came," Eli explained. "He sent me to find you and take you to the house of the shepherd Dan. His wife will prepare you for your journey."

"And what of Leah?"

"There is no need to worry for Leah. Is she not my betrothed? She will stay here as my wife."

Return without Leah? How could she endure so long a journey without the company and care of her friend?

As they hastened along, they soon came to the shepherd's hut. It looked like a deserted place. Halting at the door, Eli called softly, "I come from Ezekiel."

A woman's voice answered, "Enter. The roof of this house offers shelter to all who call Ezekiel friend."

"I bring one Miriam, daughter of Simeon."

"The one for whom Anak has come? I did not expect her so soon."

"There is trouble," Eli explained. "Evil ones would detain her. Disguise her well."

"It shall be done," the voice answered.

"She must be ready to travel before the moon has fully risen."

"It shall be so," the woman answered.

For a moment the two girls clung together in sad, loving farewell. Then Miriam was alone.

"Enter, and be not afraid," the woman invited.

Miriam took a step toward the house, but the trembling in her knees made it difficult to move.

"Quickly, child," the woman urged. "Who can say how precious each moment may be?"

"You are the one chosen to take Leah's place?" Miriam asked.

"Nay, there will be no need for such."

"No need! Who, then, is to care for my comforts and needs? It is not possible for a lady to travel without a servant!"

"Perhaps not comfortable," the woman corrected, "but possible."

"But why . . ." Miriam began, then stopped. The woman

99

had abruptly turned away. She knelt silently on the hearth, coaxing a fagot into flame. "You had best remove your garments, that we may stain your skin darker," she said.

"Stain my skin?" Miriam asked, slipping off her robe.

"Aye, it will serve you well for now. By the time it has worn off, the sun and wind will have darkened you naturally."

"Why?" Miriam wondered, as the woman poured the cool liquid over her again and again, rubbing it into her face, arms, and legs. When her body had dried, the woman brought a worn and faded tunic, the garment of a half-grown boy. Miriam asked uncertainly, "Is this the disguise of which Eli spoke?"

"Aye," the woman replied, studying her thoughtfully through half-closed eyes, "and it must be a good one. You are slight of build and your voice is low of pitch, but your hair troubles me."

"My hair?" Miriam grasped. "Oh, no, please!" But the woman seemed not to hear her as she sheared it off to a length just above Miriam's shoulders.

"You are hurting me!" Miriam cried, pressing her hands to the sides of her head.

"I am sorry if I seem rough, but the moon rises quickly and there is need for haste."

She gathered Miriam's castoff clothes into a bundle and hid them in a chest. Turning, she said, "You look like a boy, but you move and stand like a girl. There will be no time to practice, but you must remember that a boy is not bound by pretty manners, he is loose and easy."

Miriam nodded and tried to remember the sons of Jogli — their relaxed loping walk, their easy movements. Hooking one thumb beneath the braided thong that formed her girdle, she stood in a relaxed pose.

"That is good," the woman said. "Now walk."

100

As she spoke, a voice called from the darkness outside, "I come from Anak, seeking one called Benjamin."

The woman answered, "He is here," and as she said this, she thrust Miriam from the doorway. "May Jehovah go with you, Benjamin," was her brief farewell.

"Come quickly, Miriam; those who seek you draw near!" The voice was a familiar one, but Miriam had no time to wonder about it.

The man ran and walked and ran again, dragging Miriam after him. He dodged in and out among the trees, seeking a hiding place. Soon Miriam felt so exhausted that she wanted to stop to rest. Her legs no longer seemed to be a part of her body, and her chest ached so that she could scarcely breathe. She stumbled, and a sharp pain ran up her leg. She would have fallen if her guide had not caught her. In that moment, in the light of the rising moon, she saw his face. It was Asahel!

He smothered her cry of astonishment by placing his hand across her mouth. Any outcry would have betrayed them to their pursuers, who were drawing close. Asahel drew her into an opening between two houses. As they picked their way through the rubbish, it seemed to Miriam that all the filth of the village must have been deposited there.

Silently they made their way through the darkness. They left the houses and the grove behind and came, quite suddenly, up to the walls of the city. The gate loomed before them. Miriam looked up at Asahel, questioning.

"Nay," he said softly, "we enter not the city. A boatman awaits us at the river's edge."

"Soon the workmen will gather here, and Saris will question them. They will greatly frighten Leah, so that she may say too much and get herself in trouble."

"I think not, for Eli will be with her. As her husband,

he will make all answers for her — and I have no doubt that they are by now married. He will say nothing to cause us trouble."

"I was not thinking of us, but rather of those who have helped me," Miriam answered softly.

"Fret not for them. Whatever they did, they did willingly, some out of affection, and others were paid." He squeezed her fingers reassuringly. "Do not look back, Miriam. The path we walk is already yesterday, and its gates are closed against our returning. From now on you will find little comfort in thoughts of yesterday, with its luxury and easy living. Forget it, so that it may not make tomorrow's burden too hard to bear."

Miriam could hear the lap of the water and the swish of the reeds against the sides of the boat as it glided swiftly toward them. Her impulse to rush forward was firmly checked by Asahel, who whispered a warning as he pointed to a sentry striding past on the wall above. Thoroughly frightened, they stood motionless and silent, their forms fortunately blending with the shadows and the reeds. The guard, unaware of their presence, continued on his way while Miriam and Asahel, assisted by the boatman, scrambled into the boat.

"You took care of the Urash gate?" Asahel whispered.

The boatman nodded. The huge gate loomed above them, and he ordered them to lie down as the boat passed under it.

They traveled on northward, until they neared the point where the wall again met the river. A fortress stood on the eastern bank, guarding the passage. The sky was graying, and Asahel feared that the boat would be clearly visible to the sentries who stood watch. He looked inquiringly at the boatman. The man understood. "My brother went before us," he said. "He carried with him a few coins and much wine."

As they drew nearer, he added, "You must lie down in the boat and cover yourselves with the sacks. If I am challenged by anyone, I shall say that I transport cargo for one of the caravans — goods that arrived too late to be taken through the city. We do this often."

They neared the north gate and could hear the sound of the gathering caravans. "Move swifter!" Asahel urged. "We must not be late."

Annoyed by Asahel's urging, the boatman balked. "I am weary, and your pay is poor. If you would move faster, pole the boat yourself."

Asahel snorted and snatched the pole from the man's hands. He thrust it hard into the mud beneath the shallow water. Miriam clutched the sides of the boat as it lurched forward, and the man, caught suddenly off balance, fell with a splash into the water. For a moment Miriam was distressed, but Asahel assured her that the man was in no danger.

"Will he not cause us trouble?" Miriam asked.

"He might like to, but he will not. No, he will accept my gold and be satisfied. He is already in trouble with the soldiers. Such a one would not carry our story to them, even if he had not been helping us." He turned the boat and drove it hard against the bank.

As Miriam scrambled out, she could see the man running toward them, shaking his fist angrily. Asahel held up a small bag of money for him to see, then dropped it into the boat. He took Miriam's hand and together they ran along the curving base of the wall to the gate where they were to meet Anak.

The first caravan was gone when they reached the gate.

Asahel stood uncertain. When Anak saw them, he called, "You are late! Only the wiles of a balking camel have saved us this day."

When a man approached near enough to hear him, Anak turned on Miriam and scolded her. "Where have you been, you thankless child?"

Miriam, surprised and shocked at Anak's hateful attitude could think of no answer except the truth, and she was certain that she must not tell that.

"Think you that the caravan will await your pleasure?" Anak's hand shot out and slapped her sharply on the cheek. "Get you gone, you thoughtless one! Asahel has work for you to do."

Tears filled her eyes, but she would not cry. She looked up to find Asahel watching her. There was a worried frown on his face as he motioned her to follow him.

A lump of fear pushed up into her throat until it seemed that it would choke her. What was the matter with everyone? Why did Asahel wear ragged clothing and react like a slave to Anak's bidding? How had Anak dared to strike her?

When they reached the place where their animals waited, Asahel had his first opportunity to banish Miriam's fear and perplexity. "Do not hold it against Anak that he was harsh with you," he began to explain. "That, like the tunic you wear, is a part of your disguise. If he treats you too well, these men will become suspicious. Remember, we can trust no one — except each other. Always stay near to one or the other of us, that we may protect you."

There was a shout. Miriam turned to see the balking camel struggle to its feet. There was a din of shouting as the men urged their animals forward.

104

FIFTEEN

The caravan of Ephod, merchant of Rehoboth, drew to a straggling halt. Miriam sighed wearily and noted that they were again stopping at a dry camp.

They were three days out of Babylon. Miriam eased her weight from one burning foot to the other. Anak playfully scoffed at her weariness and Asahel teased her. Yet she knew that both sympathized, for Anak showed her how to rub her legs to ease the stiffness, and Asahel let her ride for part of each day. Both predicted that her muscles would soon become accustomed to the strain. She flexed her legs experimentally and smiled. She certainly was not as stiff as she had been yesterday.

Other thoughts about her improvement were interrupted by Anak's sharp order, "Come, boy! Why stand you there dreaming? Know you not that we make camp? Hurry, gather the fagots for our supper fire."

At the moment Miriam was too tired to be interested in food, but she could see that the others were already searching for fuel, and the fagots were few.

"I will tether the animals and ease their load for the night," Anak remarked to Asahel. Nodding toward Miriam he added, "Go with her, and may your company ease her weariness."

"Come, little one," Asahel called. "Let us go apart where the fagot gatherers are not so many."

One of the men smiled at them as they passed. "Going to have some help tonight, eh, Benny?" he asked.

Miriam nodded and Asahel remarked, "The day has been long, and this young fellow has been working hard at strenuous jobs all day. Work does not seem to tire him."

After they had walked some distance away from the camp, Asahel, knowing that he would not be overheard, smiled down at Miriam and remarked, "Your disguise is good. None suspect our secret."

"And you?" Miriam asked. She had been wondering about him. Was he a fugitive, too? Now she finally dared to ask, "Do you flee someone, too?"

Asahel laughed, but there was little mirth in his laughter. "I flee everyone, both the men of Nebuchadnezzar and those of Zedekiah."

"Why should you flee the men of Zedekiah? Are you not one of them?"

"Nay, not one of them. Not now."

"But you were one of the army of Zedekiah!"

"That was while I was convinced that he was the anointed, chosen to deliver Judah from the yoke of Babylon. Now I realize that Zedekiah is a mad man, the tool of wicked men. He has little thought for either Judah or Jehovah."

"Why does he hunt you?"

Asahel shrugged. "I doubt that he hunts me. He is too busy quaking in his fear as he watches Nebuchadnezzar's soldiers battering at the walls of Jerusalem. Yet I doubt not that he would like to lay his hands on me, and others like me." He bent close. "We have decided that our leadership does not lie in Zedekiah, but elsewhere."

Miriam agreed. "Jeremiah told us that Judah's future lies in Babylon."

"I cannot believe this is God's will. We are only a remnant of a nation."

106

"Have you no faith? Did not Jehovah build a nation from the sons of Jacob, even while they were slaves in Egypt?"

Asahel looked moodily out to the far horizon. After a time Miriam asked, "You do not believe the leadership lies with Zedekiah, or our destiny in Babylon. What do you believe?"

"I believe, as does your own father, that our destiny again lies in Egypt. There are many who think as we do. Some have already gone; others will follow. In that hour when Jerusalem falls, the rest of us must gather and flee."

"What does Jeremiah say?"

"He is angered and warns that Jehovah will not go with us."

She turned on him in disbelief. "And you listen not?"

"Nay, rather we believe that we are a group elected by Jehovah to rebuild the kingdom of David in all its might and glory! Think of it, Miriam, a bright new Jerusalem built on the foundations of the old, and our hands privileged to do the building!"

"I like it not!"

Asahel laughed. "Ah, little one, bother not your mind with such things. What do women know of the problems of state?"

"You listen not to the words of Jeremiah, but go into a strange land and your children will not know Jehovah!"

"Nay," Asahel denied. "When we enter Egypt, Jeremiah will go with us, and you, my beloved, will go, too."

Deciding to avoid any argument about her going with him to Egypt, she asked, "Has Jeremiah promised to do so?"

"Nay, but when the time comes, we will gather him into our midst and carry him with us."

As Miriam looked up in horrified disbelief, she suddenly

noticed Anak at the edge of the camp. He was waving at them. "Old Anak grows impatient," she said. Asahel shouldered his burden, and she silently followed him. Her heart was heavy with misgivings. For all his years, she felt older and wiser than Asahel. Somehow, before it was too late, she must make him see the error of his decision.

The evening meal was over. Miriam scoured the pot with clean sand and picked up the scraps of food and stored them away. She looked to where Asahel stood with a group of younger men. She would have liked to join them, but their talk was not for her. Turning and walking slowly to where Anak was sitting at the outer ring of the cooking fire, she sat down on the warm sand in the shadows behind him. Before long she dozed off.

Presently there was a stir at the edge of the camp. She watched sleepily as a stranger rode up to the tent of the merchant Ephod and dismounted. "I would have a word with you," he called to the guard before the entrance.

Miriam looked up questioningly at Anak and found him tense and listening.

The stranger was Saris. "I search for a maid of Judah who travels in the company of an old servant," he announced.

"None such travel here," the guard grunted.

Saris was silent, and the guard shrugged and added, "It is a large company, but I would have noticed."

"There is gold for you, should your memory improve. The maid, they say, is not hard to look upon. The old man is ugly and bent."

"But I tell you, there is no . . ." His vehement assertion was cut short by a sudden decision to try a different tack. He stepped closer to Saris. "Wait, perhaps I was wrong. What is this information worth to you?"

108

Saris raised a small bag of coins and shook it. "All are yours when you deliver the maid to me."

The bag of coins promptly improved the guard's memory. "I know them now. For some days I have sensed a strangeness in their relationship. They travel as father and son, and a young man is much in their company."

"I care not for your story; only bring the maid."

The guard nodded. "I must remain here a little longer; then I will bring her."

Miriam stepped close to Anak. "What can we do now?" she whispered.

The man beside Anak turned and looked at them closely. "It is time we took to our beds," he said loudly, Then, turning to Anak, he added softly, "Come, my friend, we will go our way together."

Miriam felt a cold chill run down her spine. This man also had heard Saris and knew their secret. When he and Anak reached the place where their beasts were tethered, Asahel was resting beside the embers of their dying fire. He got quickly to his feet and joined them.

The stranger laid a heavy hand on Anak's shoulder. "You are indeed in trouble. I have reason to know the man who entered our camp this night. It will serve me well to help you escape him."

Anak nodded slowly and asked, "You have a plan that would serve us?"

The man glanced quickly about him, then asked, "You know the caravan route?" Anak nodded and he went on, "A days' travel ahead there is a village."

"I know the place," Anak answered.

"It is good. I have two swift camels that I will lend you. Stop at the house of Enoch, the tanner, and tell him that

Hanon sent you. Remain there until I come. I will tell you whether it is safe for you to rejoin this caravan."

Anak looked up at him from beneath his heavy brows and asked, "And what of my goods and my servant?"

"I will take them with my own and return them when you return my camels."

"It is good. But what of Saris?"

"He will not find you here. Your safety will depend upon your speed, for he will follow you, but he will not find you in the house of Enoch."

Miriam waited impatiently as Anak and Asahel talked. Then they gathered up their possessions and followed Hanon to the far side of the camp, leaving her alone and un-protected.

The men had scarcely gone for the camels when an arm was slipped about Miriam's waist and a hand fastened itself across her mouth, as if to smother her. She felt herself being drawn backward, away from Hanon's camp.

She struggled, but the arm that held her only tightened its grasp. She realized that her strength was nothing as compared with his. When he attempted to shift her to a position over his left hip, she jerked back her right elbow, striking him in the stomach with all her strength. He grunted. His hold loosened for only a moment, but it was long enough for her to wrench free.

She raced ahead of him, dodging in and out among the animals. Skillfully she led him from Hanon's camp toward the camp of an old man she knew. He traveled with three burly sons. There she let the guard nearly catch her. Then, with a shriek, she dodged adroitly around a sleeping donkey while her angry pursuer thundered heedlessly straight ahead. Stumbling over the threshing legs of the frightened animal,

110

he plunged headlong down across the bodies of the startled men. During the loud and long altercation that naturally ensued, Miriam stole away and raced back to Hanon's camp, where Anak and Asahel were gravely concerned about her absence. Asahel ran to meet her.

"Where were you?" he demanded, almost dragging her to where the others waited.

"The guard!" she gasped. "We must hurry!"

Hanon nodded. "I thought as much. Go quickly, for when he returns, he will not be alone."

Miriam had been tired, but the excitement, escape, and quick departure had refreshed her. The camels were fast, as fast as Hanon had promised, and the wind whistled in her ears as they sped across the country.

It was some time after sunrise when they entered the village. Anak led the way down a narrow street of shops. He stopped before one of them and knocked for admittance. Miriam leaned down and asked softly, "Is this the house of Enoch, the tanner?"

Anak shook his head. "Nay, it is the house of a weaver named Benjamin. He once lived in Damascus and bought wool from your father. He will help us."

"But what of Hanon and his friend Enoch?"

"I am not sure about Hanon. Even now he may be plotting against us. You will be safe in the house of Benjamin. Rest and sleep until I come for you."

Miriam had scarcely dozed off when voices awakened her. "Sit down and be still! I will wash away the blood," Anak was saying. "We will save time if you talk while I work."

The voices went on, but they were lower now, and Miriam could not make out the words. She got up and went to the door to listen.

"The devil take him, for he is one of his own!" The voice was that of the weaver.

"I thought that Hanon would hide you. He seemed eager to help us," Anak mused. "He must have known that Saris would leave not a single pack unopened in his search."

"Aye, he knew." It was Asahel. "Think you that his fears for our safety equaled his desire to even his score with Saris?"

Anak sighed audibly. "Aye, I should have known. Asahel, you did well to fight Saris, but I fear his wounds will not detain him long. We must move quickly."

"Think you we can outrun him?" Asahel snorted.

"Nay, outsmart him. Your wounds look serious. Saris will expect us to hide while you rest. He will enter the village with noisy threats, and he will search every house, if necessary."

"Aye," Benjamin agreed. "Yet the town is small, and his roars may frighten some weak soul who saw you enter or leave."

"And they will point their finger at your house," Anak warned. "Therefore, you must tell him that you turned us out when you heard that we were hunted people. Be not fearful, but let your anger toward us match his own, that he be convinced."

"And what will I tell him when he asks which way you went?" Benjamin interrupted.

"Tell him that the boy is sorely wounded. We try to outwit him by seeking the shelter of the great dunes, until he, in his stupidity, will have passed along the beaten path."

Miriam closed the door and began dressing. She had scarcely finished when the wife of Benjamin opened the door and entered. "It is well that you are dressed," she said,

112

wiping her hands nervously on her robes. "Come, that you may eat and be ready when the camels are loaded. I would have you gone before the man Saris comes. I will not endanger my house further by keeping you here!"

Miriam silently followed her to the family room. The woman nodded toward a stool and handed her a bowl of hot stew and a chunk of bread. Miriam munched the bread as she waited for the stew to cool. She was not hungry, but she forced herself to chew and swallow, because it might be a long time before she again tasted food.

Asahel entered and dropped wearily onto a stool nearby. One of his eyes was blue and puffy, and his upper lip was cut and badly swollen. A wide bandage covered the lower part of his right arm. He winced a smile and she said, "I am sorry that you got hurt."

"It was a good fight. Saris fared no better," he chuckled. "I left him unconscious upon the ground. It was lucky for me that Hanon suddenly remembered that he had yet another swift camel."

Anak hurried in. He stuffed the hard bread into his girdle and drank the scalding stew. "Hurry, you two," he ordered. "The camels are ready."

They could see no sign of Saris or the caravan as they left the town. They headed north along the beaten path. When they passed the place where they were to turn off to the great dunes, Asahel asked, "Will he not notice that we left no tracks?"

"The wind would have erased them. But it will not matter. Saris' gold will loosen Benjamin's tongue if fear does not loosen it first."

Asahel turned in surprise. "Then why did you tell him of our plans?"

Anak laughed heartily. "Do you not know me better than that, my friend?" he asked. "Would I have been so free with my tongue if it was truly my plan?"

"At the time, I wondered. I thought you must know the man and trust him. It was the woman I feared."

"Aye," Anak agreed. "I but set a double trap for the dull-witted Saris."

They rode swiftly for a time; then Anak stopped and got down from his camel. He pointed to a slight rise of land. "Head for that point. When you have gone about four furlongs, stop and wait for me."

Asahel led Anak's camel as they set off. Miriam looked back and noticed that Anak had removed his mantle and followed slowly, dragging it behind him to sweep away their tracks. After traveling about a half mile, they stopped and waited for Anak, as he had instructed them.

When they reached the rise, they saw that the ground fell away sharply before them. They made their way carefully around the sand cliff. Anak ordered the camels to kneel. "We will stop here," he said.

"You know this country well," Asahel marveled.

"Aye, I searched out several such places as I journeyed down."

Miriam looked up in surprise. "How could you know that Yaama would try to detain me?"

Anak shrugged. "If it had not been Yaama, it would have been another."

"Down!" Asahel suddenly exclaimed in a loud whisper. "Two travelers come far down the beaten way."

Anak scowled thoughtfully. "It may not be Saris. I had not expected him so soon. Perhaps he did not stop to search the dunes."

"There were no tracks," Asahel reminded him.

Flat on his stomach, Anak wriggled to a point where he could watch the travelers. After a time he announced, "They go slow. It must be Saris, and the man with him knows the land well. It is fortunate that we took time to erase our tracks."

He said no more and Asahel moved nervously. "Do they pass on?" he asked anxiously.

"Nay, they search the roadway and argue."

"Could it be that they have noticed where our trail ended?" Asahel fingered the handle of a short dagger he carried in his girdle.

"Nay, a small band of soldiers left the village early this morning. Our tracks will be lost in theirs."

"Then why have they stopped there?"

"Is it impossible that the one who travels with him also knows we could find shelter here?" Anak replied with ill-concealed impatience. Observing the travelers closely for a few minutes more, he saw that they were continuing along the road. Then he announced with a sigh of relief, "They mount and ride on!"

He watched them out of sight before returning to where Miriam and Asahel waited. "We will rest here until darkness," he said.

Asahel nodded soberly, and Miriam looked from one to the other, wondering. Certainly Anak did not mean that they were going to set off alone across the vast, trackless desert with only the stars to guide them! She looked at the pack camels and noted the waterskins and the provisions. The answer was clear. But there was another question. "Saris? Will he not turn back when he does not find us?" she asked.

Anak laughed. "He will hope to overtake us before nightfall. When he does not, he will be too weary to do anything but rest. Tomorrow we are gone."

SIXTEEN

After their early breakfast, Miriam stood up to scan the desert expanse, but all she could see was sand, with an occasional tuft of yellowed vegetation. She brushed the hair from her face and stooped to gather up the remaining scraps of their morning meal.

Anak had thought to reach an oasis by this morning. What would happen if they had passed it in the darkness? Would they have food and water until they reached another?

"Look, already Anak sleeps," Asahel noted, stretching tall before dropping down on the warm sand. "He is old. I fear the journey overtires him. Perhaps I should let him sleep longer today."

"Could I not watch for a while?"

"Nay, though I would like it well if you sat for a while and talked with me."

She sat down beside him and yawned. As she slumped forward, supporting her chin on her up-drawn knees, she remarked, "This journey is endless!"

Asahel chuckled. "Nay. It is only the sameness of the days that makes it seem so, but it will not be too much longer now. The next oasis will be the last, for in a few days we leave the desert lands."

Miriam scratched her chin thoughtfully against the roughness of her tunic. "It is not much like my journey into Babylon. You should have heard us fretting over the hardships of that journey! Leah liked not the nights we could not spend at some inn."

116

Asahel looked up and nodded. "You miss Leah, do you not?"

She nodded. "Of course, but I know she is happier where she is. I find it hard to think of Leah with a husband."

Asahel watched her closely as she spoke. "Does it seem odd to you that soon we shall be wed also?"

"When I saw how happy Leah was when Eli was near, I envied her. Then I would remember that I, too, am betrothed, but my feelings for you seemed so different." She paused and casually wound the ends of her girdle about her waist. She found it difficult to choose words that would express her feelings. "Then we met in Ephram's garden and I realized that my feelings for you were really like Leah's." She looked up at him, searching his face, to see whether he understood what she was trying to tell him.

Asahel reached out and took her hand. "I'm glad," he said softly. He moved closer and put his arm around her.

The travelers passed south of the Dead Sea, through the wadi of Arabah and northwestward to Arad. Anak left Miriam and Asahel at a small inn at the edge of the village. When he returned, he brought donkeys and provisions which he received in exchange for their camels.

Travel was easier now, and Miriam was filled with a restless impatience to be home with her parents, especially after she saw here and there some familiar sights of her homeland. There were questions she wanted to ask, but Anak was irritable and Asahel, she noticed, was in no mood for talk. He seemed to be troubled about some matter which, for the time being, he did not wish to share with her.

Miriam's first view of her home was not a happy one. It had a deserted look. She was seized by the fear that they were already too late. Was her father already dead and her mother carried off by some passing Babylonian soldier?

She was blinking hard to hold back her tears. When they turned aside and made their way upward into the hills, she did not need to ask where they were going. She knew.

A call broke the silence of the hills around them. Miriam looked up and saw a figure standing on a high rock, waving.

"Fool!" Anak exclaimed angrily.

"Be not cross with him," Asahel chided. "His watch has likely been long. He could not mistake us for other than what we are."

Anak snorted. "How can we know that there are not other ears to hear him?"

Asahel shrugged and they went on in silence till they came to the shepherd's hut.

Melia, the wife of Jogli, was bending over a small cooking fire. She looked up, startled, as they approached. Then her worried expression broke into a smile. "Long have we waited for your return!" she cried. Miriam responded with a warm smile, but she had no time for words.

She hurried on to the cave. Her mother met her at the entrance. "It is so good to be back!" Miriam cried, throwing her arms around her mother. She felt safe and protected again. She was home.

She was surprised at the tired lines on her mother's face and, remembering her father, asked, "Is he no better?"

"Come and see," her mother replied, as they walked slowly to where he lay. Miriam stood looking down at him for a long time. Surely this gaunt, white-haired old man could not be her father!

"You have returned," he said without opening his eyes. At the sound of his voice she could no longer doubt.

As he held her hand, she sat for a long time, telling them of the things which she had seen and answering their many questions. Then Melia came and took her to a place which had been prepared for her comfort. As she bathed

118

and dressed, she could hear the men arguing in the outer room. She paused as she heard a well-remembered voice, the voice of Jeremiah.

A worried frown settled over Melia's face. "They are at it again!" she muttered. "They curse Zedekiah that he listened not to Jeremiah, yet they will not listen themselves."

"Come, I will help you with their supper," Miriam said, stooping to tie the thong of her sandal. "Men are always more quarrelsome when they are hungry."

It was dark by the time they were all fed. Miriam entered the cave and sat down at her mother's side. She was very tired, but she wanted to hear what the men had to say.

She had nearly dozed off when their angry voices aroused her. Jeremiah was pacing angrily back and forth. He peered first at one and then another. "Are you all mad that you refuse to listen?" he demanded. "Once more I will tell you. Thus said the Lord: 'Like these good figs, so will I regard the captives of Judah, whom I have sent out of this place into the land of the Chaldeans, for good. I will set mine eyes upon them for good, and I will bring them again into this land: and I will give them a heart to know me, that I am Jehovah: and they shall be my people and I will be their God; for they shall return unto me with their whole heart.

"And as for the bad figs which cannot be eaten, so will I give up Zedekiah, the king of Judah, and his princes, and the residue of Jerusalem, that remain in this land, AND THEM THAT DWELL IN THE LAND OF EGYPT. I will even give them up to be tossed to and fro among all the nations of the earth for evil; to be a reproach and a proverb, a taunt and a curse, in all places whither I shall drive them; and I will send the sword and famine, and pestilence, among

119

them, till they are consumed from off the land that I gave unto them and to their fathers."

Miriam listened and trembled. How could her father and Asahel refuse to heed these words?

A frightening silence settled over the group. Miriam stole a glance to where her father lay. His face was gray and expressionless. A coarse robe brushed against her arm. She turned to watch Jeremiah hurry from the chamber. The nervous trembling within her increased until it seemed that she could no longer breathe. She got quietly to her feet and went outdoors.

Jeremiah stood a short distance from the entrance. He was looking heavenward. "He is talking with Jehovah," Miriam thought. Silently she walked to the flat rocks and sat down. She remembered the day that she and Asahel had discovered the cave. Leah had been with them. Sudden loneliness for her friend brought tears to her eyes.

"Is the burden of their decision so heavy upon your heart, my child?" Jeremiah asked softly.

Miriam looked up. For a moment she had forgotten Jeremiah and his words. Now she remembered. "Why will they not listen?" she asked.

"You have listened and you have understood. Perhaps that is enough."

Miriam tried to see his face in the darkness. Surely, at such a time, he would not laugh at her. "I am only a girl," she answered. "What my heart understands will make no difference. Where my father leads, there must I go. And after my father there will be my husband." She shook her head sadly. "Nay, Jeremiah, do not mock me, for I need your comfort."

"I do not mock you. A woman has great power. More than one has swayed the minds of the men she loved — some for good, some for evil."

120

Miriam looked down at the clenched hands in her lap. "What must I do?" she asked.

Jeremiah laid his hand in benediction upon her head. "Speak softly, be kind, be loving, above all be obedient, but never forget your convictions. I go, but I will return again to plead with them."

She waited for him to say more. When he did not, she looked up and found that he was gone, but her mother was moving slowly toward her through the darkness.

"Do not let their words frighten you," she said softly. "It is the way of men to argue."

"I fear not their arguing, Mother. It is their decision that I fear. What is to become of us?"

"Worry not your heart over that, my daughter. Your father is a wise and good man. He will lay his plans well." She put an arm around Miriam's shoulders and drew her close.

"But I fear," Miriam insisted.

"The decision must be theirs, Miriam. As women, we are not expected to understand."

Miriam drew away and looked up into her mother's face. "If the choice were yours, where would you go?"

Her mother shrugged. "The choice is not mine; it is my husband's. Where he leads I will follow, for he is my wisdom. It is the basic rule of life. Is it not better that I set aside the words I hear, and think only of his needs and how I may comfort him?"

Miriam sat silent for a time, then asked bitterly, "If it is wrong for a woman to think, why did God give her a mind?"

"Speak not angrily of your fate! Rather, thank the God of our fathers that the decision need not be yours." She turned and, lifting Miriam's chin, looked long and deeply into her moon-lit face. "You have been too long away from your people. I know not what they have taught you in that strange land. But this I do know: My husband is my lord and yours, his wish is our command."

SEVENTEEN

All was dark, except for a flickering pool of light around Simeon's bed. Miriam leaned over her father to straighten the robe that covered him. Each day he seemed weaker, and each night his sleep was more restless, as the illness ate away at his strength. There was a strange roughness in his breathing, and for a time he seemed to stop breathing entirely. Miriam held her own breath, listening. Then, with a deep sigh, he began again.

Behind the curtain that shut off the far end of the chamber, Asahel slept. He had come in at nightfall, too tired even to eat.

There was a faint rustle in the passageway. Miriam listened. "Anak?" she called softly.

A moment of tense silence followed. Then, "Nay, daughter of Simeon, not Anak."

She turned eagerly. "Jeremiah!" she exclaimed. "You have returned sooner than I expected."

"You are alone?" He moved slowly to the bed where her father lay. Stooping, he lifted one limp hand while looking intently at the man.

"Nay," Miriam answered. "Asahel has just returned. He sleeps. My mother sleeps also."

122

"It is good that Asahel has returned, for I would speak with him again while there is yet time."

Miriam looked up, startled by the sadness in his voice.

Jeremiah raised himself slowly to his full height and laid a hand upon her head in blessing. "Aye, little one," he said, "the time grows short. Tomorrow I go up to Jerusalem."

"You have said we must not go to Egypt," she said softly. "Yet, many feel Jehovah will again make a nation of Israel within those boundaries."

"Is slavery in Egypt to be desired above slavery in Babylon?"

"We would not be slaves in Egypt. My father has stored much wealth there."

"I understand but one thing, my child, and it is this: Jehovah has spoken and He has said, 'Go to Babylon.'"

Miriam shuddered as his voice echoed through the room. She fell on her knees before him. "What must I do?" she asked.

Her father stirred and opened his eyes. "Do, my daughter?" he asked softly. Then he added, "Honor thy father and obey thy husband in all things, for that is the law."

She looked from her father to Jeremiah. "Jeremiah says that Jehovah has ordered that all Judah must go to Babylon. You, my father, say that it is God's will that we go to Egypt."

"Silence!" Simeon gasped angrily. "Do you question my wisdom?" He shook his head sadly. "I fear that a stronger hand than mine is needed to guide you. Tomorrow we will make preparations for you to wed Asahel."

"Father! It is still not too late! Perhaps if you and Asahel . . ."

"I have spoken!" Simeon interrupted her angrily. "Tomorrow we will begin our preparations."

"Nay!" a voice interposed.

Miriam turned to find Asahel standing just outside the ring of light.

Simeon looked up in surprise. "What say you, Asahel?" he demanded.

"There will be no marriage preparations. Think you I want for wife one whose heart lies elsewhere?" He shook his head as though to clear away the dizziness of sleep. "In these perilous times, a man needs a wife who will be faithful to him and accept his authority and beliefs without question."

"And you think Miriam will not do this?"

"Has she not already, before witnesses, questioned our authority?" He paused looking down at her. "Or is it rather, that she would return to Babylon because she prefers the man Urusar to me?"

For a time there was silence in the cave, broken only by the rasp of Simeon's breathing. He lay silent and exhausted, with eyes closed. Slowly he turned and opened his eyes. "Is this true, my daughter?"

"Nay, my father. The nephew of Nebuzaradan is no more than a good friend to me."

"Can you deny that he holds you in deep affection, or that there is a promise between you?" Asahel challenged.

"This is a serious charge that you make, Asahel," Simeon said slowly, "one that I find hard to believe."

"Three days back, I was captured as a spy and delivered to the tent of Nebuzaradan. The man Urusar ordered that I be released and walked with me to the edge of the encampment. When I asked why, he said that he had so promised the sweet lady Miriam."

"What say you to this?" Simeon asked, looking up at Miriam.

"Urusar once promised that he would bring Asahel safely to me, but there is no other promise between us. It is

124

his way of repaying me for the friendship I gave his sister Abilath. He knows we are betrothed, Asahel, and he promised to protect you."

"I need not his protection!"

Simeon shook his head thoughtfully. "Already Urusar's friendship seems to have served you well, my son. Who knows, perhaps it may again." He closed his eyes.

Miriam could not look up into the faces of Jeremiah and Asahel. Shame filled her thoughts. Could it be that Asahel would really disgrace her by setting her aside? She waited for him to speak, but he turned and silently returned to his bed.

Jeremiah laid a hand upon her shoulder. "I doubt not that he will relent. He is overtired now," he said. The prophet stood beside Miriam for a time, stroking her hair comfortingly.

Miriam went to bed, determined that she would talk with Asahel in the morning, when he was rested. But, when morning came, both Asahel and Anak were gone. It was nearing dusk when Anak returned. He dropped down on the floor beside Simeon's bed, with a weary grunt.

"You are late!" Simeon greeted him impatiently.

"Aye. We had to wait while scouts passed."

"Our friends are ready to leave?" Simeon asked.

"At the setting of the sun." Anak looked sharply at Miriam. "I would speak with your father alone."

She nodded her obedient response. She would have liked to listen. She wondered what new plans they were making. At the door she met Asahel entering.

Miriam knew that Anak and Asahel had been at the cave which was an hour's journey to the south, where small groups gathered for their journey to Egypt. These people were their greatest source of news. Miriam frowned as she joined her mother and Melia. Both Anak and Asahel had been extremely grave. It must have been grim news that they heard today.

It was not until she took in their supper that she knew how serious it was. As she entered the room, Anak was saying, "The walls cannot stand more than a few days longer."

"You must go with this caravan," Simeon urged.

"Nay, there will be others later, when you are stronger," Anak said.

"I grow weaker. You had better go without me while there is yet time."

"Rather," Asahel suggested, "let us go up into the hills outside the city, that we may see for ourselves what is happening."

Simeon nodded. "The boy speaks wisely."

Miriam had been listening intently. Now she asked, "May I go with them, Father?"

Simeon turned, surprised by her interruption. "You? Nay, my daughter. It is no place for a girl."

Asahel's eyes glared slightly at Miriam as he said, "Perhaps it might be well if she went. Let her see the destruction wrought by the Babylonians. Then, perhaps, she will understand why we go to Egypt."

Simeon lay back, his eyes closed in thought. "I do not know," he said. "I like it not."

Miriam shuddered regretfully. She had spoken on an impulse. Now she realized that it had been unwise. Her father opened his eyes and looked at her. "Take her, let her see," he said.

It was nearly daylight of the second day before they came in sight of the city. They heard the thunder of the battering rams and saw the red reflection of the fire against the sky from many miles away. They climbed up to a point where they could see the city in the distance.

When daylight came, the red faded from the sky and a huge canopy of black smoke, laced with flame, took its place. Arrows with flaming tips arched through the sky and into the city. There were many fires within the walls. Miriam could not believe her own eyes. Everything seemed impossible and unreal to her. She tried to fit Urusar and his uncle into the picture, but she could not.

"I have seen enough!" Asahel said abruptly.

Turning to Miriam, he demanded, "What think you now of those whom you would call friend?"

Miriam looked up into the cold hatred that distorted his face. It was not the Asahel she knew. She was afraid. "I know not," she gasped.

"Then it is time you decided!"

"Aye, we must turn back now," Anak tactfully suggested. "This is no sight for the child's eyes."

"And what of those women and children behind the walls?" Asahel demanded. There was a sob in his words as he hurried on ahead of them.

The people? Miriam had not thought of the people within those walls. Suddenly she was sick with the thought of their suffering — the suffering of all Judah. A prayer for deliverance rose within her until it tingled through her entire being, like a long, thin cry. She steeled herself against her trembling, but she could not silence the echoing of that desperate cry. How often had Jehovah heard it echoing through the ages, she wondered. Had Abraham so cried while traveling through the far reaches of a strange land? Had the sons of Israel cried that same cry as they staggered beneath the yoke of Egypt?

She could hardly bear to look at the terrifying scene below. Almost numb with fright and pity, she turned her back on the flaming city. Again the cry rose within her.

She knew that her cry was one with the cry of all her people, a bond between them and their God.

"Jehovah protect them," old Anak said, as though he could read her thoughts. He took her hand and led her down a rocky defile, Asahel sulkily following.

All the way home Miriam tried to place Nebuzaradan, her kindly and considerate host in Babylon, in the role of the one who had planned such destruction, but she could not. Nor could she understand Asahel's surly silence. Somehow he seemed to hold her personally responsible for what was happening at Jerusalem.

Obed, the son of Jogli, ran down the trail to meet them. Miriam knew, even before he spoke, that he carried bad news. "The master lies near to death," he gasped.

Anak stopped to question the boy, but Miriam ran ahead of the others. She scarcely noticed when she stumbled and fell, skinning one knee. Her only thought was that she should never have gone on this strange journey. She should have been here at her father's bedside, helping her mother.

Miriam walked slowly past her sobbing mother and bent over her father's bed. Anak and Asahel joined her. Anak put a comforting arm about her shoulders. "Weep not for him, little one. A few hours, a few days, and he will be released from his suffering."

EIGHTEEN

Melia wept bitterly. She was torn between two strong loyalties — to stay with Simeon, her husband's master, or to go to Babylon, her daughter Leah's home. "It is not right," she sobbed, "that I should leave your mother, especially now with the master so ill!"

"Be still, woman! Is it not by your own choice that we go the Babylon way?" Jogli demanded.

Miriam lovingly patted Melia's plump shoulder. She had a wild impulse to cry out that she would go with them, but she set her lips tight to hold back the words.

Asahel watched her closely. He demanded angrily, "Why do you not say that their choice is the wise one and that you wish we were all going with them to Babylon?"

Melia shot him an angry glance and turned back to Miriam. "Who will do for your mother and you when I am gone?" she asked, daubing at her eyes with the hem of her scarf.

Miriam attempted a reassuring smile in spite of her sorrow at parting. "Fear not for us. What we cannot do, Anak and Asahel will help us to do. I learned to do many things on my journey home." She was pleased by the steadiness of her voice.

Melia gave her an answering smile with a few tears in it. Then she stooped to gather up the bundles which she must carry.

While she was watching Melia, Miriam did not notice that Anak and Asahel were also preparing to leave. They had made no mention of going; they never did. Often they left with the rising of the sun, to return long after its setting — and there were the times when they had not returned for many days. Her mother never asked where they were going. It would never have occurred to her to ask, for it was man's business, not woman's.

"Watch your father well, and stay out of sight." Anak instructed Miriam as he secured his knife in his girdle.

It was nearing noon when Simeon awoke and asked for water. The small jug beside his bed was empty. Miriam took it to the large jug, that she might fill it. The earth around the large jug was wet. She stooped and ran her hand along the outside of the jar. There was a large crack near the base. Quickly she tipped it up, drained out the little that remained, and carried it to her father.

"I must go for more water," she said quietly to her mother.

"Nay, but the jug is already full," her mother insisted.

"It was full, but it has drained away."

Her mother went quickly to inspect the jar. She returned, frowning. "I do not like to have you go, but your father will need water to drink."

Miriam hurried down the path toward the well. It was a cool day. She paused to pick one of the flowers that grew from between the rocks. Then she remembered her errand and hurried on.

She had walked only a few steps when she was startled and frightened by voices. She looked cautiously around, but she could see no one. She left the path and made her way to a place where the rocks that jutted out of the hillside were larger. Slowly she climbed up to a point where she could see far out across the level plain below. Several horses stood around the well and men with them.

A man stepped from the house and called, "There is no one here. I told you that it was deserted."

"Then we must seek them out."

Miriam gasped and drew back into the shelter of the rock. The second voice was Urusar's.

She watched as they held a hurried conference and then fanned out to search the area. As they drew near her hiding place, she let herself down into the crevice between two rocks. The sound of the voices came closer. "It is evident that they have been gone for some time," a man said.

"But someone lives near." It was Urusar. "Did you not

notice the well? It is used regularly. Also, there were foot-prints in the sand around it."

"Would it not be easier to guard the well? Then you could question whoever came."

"Nay. I know the man Simeon. I would offer him pro-tection."

The voices faded away. Miriam wanted to call to Urusar and lead him to her father, but she feared that he would take him away, and, besides, her father was too ill to travel. And what of Asahel? If she spoke now with Urusar, Asahel would never believe in her again.

She raised her head. There was no one in sight. She looked toward the spring, where the horses waited. There was no soldier there, but she could not be certain that there was not one close by. It would not be safe for her to get the water. Slowly she followed the men up the path. There was a call from one far ahead, "I have found a second path."

"Aye," called another, "and I have found a place where someone has camped. These ashes cannot be over a day old."

Miriam held her breath and listened. She feared that their shouts would awaken her father and that he would call out, thinking that Anak and Asahel had returned.

"Come, the path goes on," another called.

Miriam followed at a safe distance. When she saw her chance, she darted into the cave. Her mother looked up as she entered. "I feared for your safety."

"There was no need for you to fear. They meant no harm."

"You knew them?"

Miriam nodded. "It was Urusar. He had come to offer us his protection."

"You spoke with him?"

"Nay, but I heard them talking."

Her father had been watching her closely. Now he closed

131

his eyes, and she thought that he was sleeping, until he said, "It is well, for now I know that you spoke truly when you said that he was no more than a friend to you." He opened his eyes long enough to smile up at her and to say, "I no longer fear to leave you, for I know where your heart lies." He did not open his eyes again, not even when Asahel and Anak returned after their unexplained absence.

NINETEEN

Simeon was dead. Miriam stood silent beside her mother. Her eyes were wide and dry, smarting with unshed tears. A great lump filled her throat. It seemed hours since Anak and Asahel had carried her father back into this narrow opening and she had joined her mother in preparing for his burial. She could hear the men talking. She could not understand what they said, yet, somehow, she knew, for there was no longer any need to delay their departure. Asahel would be saying that they had already delayed too long their exodus to Egypt.

Miriam shivered when she recalled that Jeremiah had said that Jehovah would not march with those who went to Egypt. Why had Asahel set his face toward Egypt with a stubbornness that would not let him turn aside?

The air was heavy with the perfume of oil and spice. Miriam longed for the fresh air outside. Her mother turned and patted her cheek. "You may go now, I will follow soon," she said.

Miriam stumbled back to the main room of the cave and

dropped down on a seat near the door. She closed her eyes and breathed deeply.

"Why sit you there idle, child?" Anak demanded.

"Be not harsh with her," Asahel said kindly. "It is only right that she should have her hour of grief. Simeon was a good father, and wise."

"Think you that I do not also grieve?" Anak asked sharply. "But the dead are now buried and our thoughts must turn to the living." He paused and frowned. "Already we have tarried overlong."

Miriam rose and walked to a large, hollow slab of stone. She poured a measure of wheat onto it and began to pound and grind the meal for the evening cakes.

"The hour grows late and we hunger!" Anak grumbled. "Have you no meal in readiness?"

Miriam blinked hard to hold back her tears, but they fell from her lashes and made tiny splashes on the rock. Anak was being cross. It helped little to know that it was his own sense of loss and grief that made him so.

"Do not cry, Miriam," Asahel said softly. "Give me the stone and I will grind while you stir the fire."

Miriam looked up and tried to smile, but instead she sobbed, "Oh, Asahel, why must we go to Egypt? Can you not find it in your heart to listen to Jeremiah?"

Asahel flushed, and his eyes flashed with quick anger. "Why do you always question my decisions!" he complained.

Miriam looked up and wondered at the heat of his sudden anger. Could it be that he was beginning to doubt his judgment. "Do you not at times fear the punishment that Jeremiah prophesies for those who do not obey the commands of Jehovah?" she asked meekly.

"Enough! You are free to go where your heart dictates."

Miriam looked up at him in stunned disbelief.

Anak said, "Think well, my son, before you take so harsh a step."

"I but free her to go where she wishes!" Asahel replied sharply. "How can a man take for wife a woman who will dictate his decisions even before they are married?"

When neither said more, Miriam looked up, begging for understanding. "In the night," she began softly, "it seems that I hear a voice calling and always it asks, 'Why will you not heed my voice?'"

"It is only a dream," Asahel retorted.

Anak asked, "Why said you nothing of this?"

"I would not give my father cause for more worry," she answered.

Anak nodded thoughtfully. "Of late, I have had little liking for the way we go. The words of Jeremiah prey upon my mind also. I ask myself whether it would not be better if we listened to him."

Asahel looked from one to the other, and Miriam could again sense his uncertainty. "It is still not too late to reconsider," she urged.

"Nay!" He shook his head stubbornly. "It is by my counseling that others have gone to Egypt. Would it not seem strange if I now went the other way?"

Anak shook his head. "Nay. Your responsibility is to yourself and to Miriam. Every man must assume his own responsibility for the way he goes."

"I cannot believe that Jehovah again sends Israel into slavery!" Asahel replied. "Our nation is already reduced to the place where it may easily be lost in the hardships of slavery."

"And if it is Jehovah's will, think you He cannot preserve His people?" Anak demanded. "Not only will He preserve them, but in the fullness of time He will bring them forth

134

again and back to this land which He has given them. They will rebuild the walls of Jerusalem and reconstruct His temple."

Miriam looked up at Anak in wonder. Truly, he must have changed his mind.

"I know not what to believe," Asahel said to Anak. "You are free to go where you will. Since your heart lies in Babylon, take Miriam with you. Take her to the tent of Nebuzaradan."

Miriam looked up. She must have misunderstood what he said. "Nay, Asahel," she cried. "I must go where you go. It has been so destined. If I have angered you, forgive me."

"Do you think it is easy for me that we go two ways?" he asked.

Miriam turned away to hide her tears. How could she bear to lose both her father and Asahel? "Come with us," she pleaded. "Think of the things which Jeremiah has told us." When he did not answer, she turned to face him. "Please Asahel, we need you!" Then feeling suddenly shy, she added softly, "Judah needs you, Asahel. My father has often said that you were very wise for one so young."

"I know not what to say."

Anak turned to Miriam and asked, "Have you ever doubted as to this way we go?"

Miriam shook her head. "Nay, since first Jeremiah gave us the message, I have known."

"Only a woman who is following her heart knows no doubts!" Asahel interrupted angrily.

"You admit, then, that you have doubted?"

"I do not deny that at times I have doubted. Do not all men at times doubt both their abilities and their wisdom?"

"All men doubt their own wisdom and abilities," Anak agreed. "The truly wise pray for guidance and meditate."

135

"You think I have not prayed?" Asahel asked. His shoulders slumped wearily, and Miriam would have liked to comfort him, but she made no move.

"Well I know you have prayed for guidance," Anak answered, "but have you also listened for instructions, or have you gone your own stubborn way?"

"I have tried," Asahel said thoughtfully. "How can one tell how much of what he hears in his heart is Jehovah's will and how much is his own stubborn determination?" He looked searchingly at the old man, but Anak was silent.

Breaking the silence which followed, Asahel said, "I must have time to consider these things which we have said."

"Your supper!" Miriam interrupted. "Certainly you need not leave until you have eaten!"

Neither of the men seemed to hear her. As Asahel spoke his brusque farewell, Anak said, "We will wait until high noon. If you have not returned, we will go on alone."

TWENTY

The day was no more than a patch of gray against the eastern sky when Miriam made her way to the entrance of the cave. She stood looking about her, in unreasoning fear. She had just awakened, and when she noticed that Anak was also gone, she was at first not unduly alarmed.

Reason told her that he would soon return, that he had very likely only gone to the well for water, or he might be searching for Asahel. Reason told her that he would never leave them, but only yesterday no one could have told her that Asahel would set her aside. But he had.

Slowly she let her hands fall to her sides. She took several deep breaths of fresh air and turned back into the cave. She would awaken her mother, but she must say nothing that would add to her burden of sorrow and worry.

"We must prepare a hearty meal for when the men return," her mother said.

Miriam smiled, remembering other mornings when, having been out all through the night, they had returned with a great hunger.

At midmorning, her mother's brother Leban with his wife, Ruth, and his children arrived for a brief stop at the cave. They were on their way to the gathering place. "Come, my sister," he said after greeting her, "my heart is filled with many things which I would say to you privately."

Miriam watched them disappear into the cave. Ruth sat on one of the flat rocks, weeping. The children looked around with wide, frightened eyes. After a time, Leban and her mother reappeared. Her mother carried her bundle of clothing, her uncle a sack of meal. Leban tossed the sack of grain across one of his donkeys. "Your father is dead," he said, turning to Miriam. "I am now your guardian, and as such I have the right to insist that your marriage is to take place this night, before we leave."

"My mother, will she not go with us?"

"It is best this way, my daughter," her mother answered. "I am a widow. I will re-enter my father's household, and Leban is now the head of that house. I will be useful there. I can help Ruth with the children during our journey."

Miriam clung to her mother in a tight embrace. How could she tell her of the plans they had made? "We will go on ahead," her mother was saying. "You must wait for

Asahel and Anak, that you may tell them. May Jehovah bless you and keep you."

Blinking back her tears, Miriam watched them until they disappeared behind a hill. Even after she could no longer see them, she remained standing — and thinking. How could she cut herself off from all those she loved?

It was nearly noon, but neither Anak nor Asahel had returned. Miriam climbed to the lookout rock. She could see far in every direction, but she could not see a living creature. The sun beat warm against her back, but she did not feel it through her terrifying sense of aloneness. What should she do?

Last night she had been so certain that she was right. When Asahel left, she had been sure that by daybreak he would be back. But he had not returned, and Anak was also gone. "What shall I do?" she whispered to the wind. She was alone, and she was deep in trouble.

Somewhere to the south were the caves where her mother and Leban waited. She wondered whether Asahel was there with them. Would he be pleased if she joined them? Would he even marry her, as her father had planned? She thought of the life of comfort they would live in Egypt, with the wealth her father had laid up for them there. She weighed it against the slavery of Babylon. She was a woman; was it not her duty to do as her father had decreed? Had she a right to stand against him?

But what of the wrath of Jehovah, of which Jeremiah spoke. What of His promises?

She turned slowly and made her way downward to the cave. At the entrance she thought, "I must pray to Jehovah, that He guide me."

Having made her decision she gathered her possessions into a bundle and shook out the tunic she had worn on her

138

return journey from Babylon. It would serve her well if she traveled alone.

She dressed quickly and made her way back to the main room of the cave. Her hair had grown and she must cut it. She looked down at her hands and arms. There would be no need for dyes this time. The rough life of her journey home had weathered her skin and there had been little thought, or time, in her life since, to turn them soft and white again.

Miriam worked quickly, forgetting everything but her need to disguise herself well. While she was preoccupied with these preparations, she was startled by a familiar voice. "It is well that you prepare yourself."

Turning quickly about, she saw Anak standing at the entrance. Instantly she rushed toward and threw her arms around him, sobbing, "O Anak, You have returned! I feared that you too had deserted me!"

"Nay, dry your eyes and wait upon me, for I hunger." He patted her shoulder soothingly. "You should have known that I was but searching out the way we must go."

He glanced around the room. "Asahel? Has he not returned?"

"Nay. He is likely even now with the others."

Anak frowned. "I just came from there. I saw your mother and your uncle, too. They leave this night at sundown."

"You told them that we will not be going with them?"

"I told them only that I was not going. It pleased them not. They called me traitor and drove me from among them."

"It is not right that they should treat you so!" Miriam cried indignantly.

"It is no more than I would have done, had I been in their place. But what of Asahel?"

"Do you fear that they will turn against him also?"

"Nay, I spoke for myself only."

Miriam blinked back her tears. She knew now that he did not believe that Asahel would return.

Anak, watching her, asked, "You have not changed your mind, daughter of Simeon?"

She shut her mind to thoughts of Asahel and of her mother. "Nay, Jehovah has willed it so and I will go."

TWENTY-ONE

It was the twenty-ninth day of the fourth month. It was twenty days since the flight of Zedekiah from the city of Jerusalem. Already the people of Judah were being herded into a camp situated on the plains that spread between Gibeon and Ramah.

Miriam and Anak circled east of Jerusalem. They paused at a point from which they could view the ruins. Shocked at the sight, Miriam lamented, "The desolation of it is as the desolation of Israel; its suffering, the suffering of Israel."

She turned to find that Anak had covered his face with his hands and stood swaying slowly back and forth. She could not tell whether he was weeping or praying.

They walked on in silence. Miriam paused to glance back over her shoulder for one last look at the ruined city. "Look not back, my child," Anak said with a deep sigh. "Jerusalem is fallen. Rather look ahead to that day when Jehovah will restore her."

"I have heard that Jerusalem was not a beautiful city.

140

Think you that we will restore it in the likeness and beauty of Babylon?" Miriam asked.

"Nay, for the beauty of Babylon is like unto that of a beautiful and wicked woman who uses her beauty for man's destruction. Her beauty lies in the parks and temples of her false gods and the luxury of houses filled with slaves."

"And Jerusalem? What was it like?"

"Jerusalem had a quiet beauty that impressed the soul, not the eye, a beauty that warmed the heart and fed the spirit," he answered.

"Yaama said that it was a collection of huts surrounded by a wall."

"So it would have seemed to Yaama."

"Yet Asahel thought it beautiful and exciting."

"Aye, and I too," Anak agreed.

Her thoughts wandered from the city to the people who had lived there. Perhaps some now lived in the camp near Ramah. Turning to Anak, she asked, "What think you has happened to Zedekiah and his princes?"

"There are many rumors, but I know not the truth of them. Some say he has fled into Egypt, others that he is a prisoner and that his sons are now dead."

Miriam nodded thoughtfully. "Once Asahel said that he was a mad man. He must have been mad not to listen to Jeremiah."

"Aye, to us it is madness. But what is madness, and who of us can judge him?" Anak shrugged. "Always he was surrounded by false friends. But it matters little that Zedekiah went his own way, for has not Jehovah promised that He will again draw Judah unto Himself?"

They picked their way cautiously around the camp of the Babylonian soldiers and traveled on northward. It was a journey of about five miles from Jerusalem to the edge of the camp.

When they sighted the camp, they left the beaten track and traveled on to a place where they could see the outskirts of the camp without being noticed. Miriam lowered her bundle to the ground and rubbed her aching muscles. "What do we do now?" she asked.

Anak grunted wearily. He settled himself upon the ground beside his pack before answering, "We will wait here and watch the others that come, to see what they do. At nightfall we will enter the camp and search for Jogli."

"Melia will be here," Miriam said, relieved by the knowledge that she would not be alone.

The day was already far spent and they could see a few women bending over a cooking fire at the outer fringes of the camp. Miriam watched them intently, wondering whether one of them might not be Melia.

When loud cries interrupted her thoughts, she turned and saw a group of people approaching along the road. Several Babylonian soldiers were with them, prodding them to greater speed. Anak sighed and shook his head. Miriam asked impatiently, "Why must they weep so?"

Anak turned and looked at her searchingly. "Do you feel no sadness that you must leave the land of your birth and live out your days in a strange country?"

"Aye, but what good does it do to weep? Will tears change the will of Jehovah? Will they rebuild the walls of Jerusalem?" she demanded. "No wonder the guards prod them! Their weeping shames Jehovah and Judah!"

"And you, daughter of Simeon?"

"When I enter the camp I will go proudly. Am I not a daughter of Judah, one of the chosen people of Jehovah?"

"Are you forgetting, little one, that we even now go to surrender ourselves as slaves?" Anak asked soberly.

"Nay, I have not forgotten," she answered decisively,

"but rather I would remember that my captivity is the will of Jehovah, and that He is a just and righteous God."

Anak agreed that she was right.

Miriam turned back to watching the camp. She had wanted to suggest to Anak that they seek out Nebuzaradan, but she remembered that it was not wise for a woman to question the decisions of the men of her household.

Looking around, she found the old man slumped down in a sound sleep. She knew that he would want her to awaken him, but he had gone without sleep for a long time. Certainly there could be no harm in letting him sleep for an hour, while she watched. The thought pleased her. Furthermore, it gave her another opportunity to observe the activity within the camp.

While she was silently watching the camp, her misery descended more closely about her. There was no happiness in this journey. How different it was from the first time she had gone to Babylon. Then she had gone eagerly, looking forward to the happy weeks that the prospect promised. Nor was it like the hard trip home. Asahel had been with them then — happy and surly by turn, but always there.

She could see no happiness ahead, only the harsh reality of Judah's slavery, barren of all those she loved best. It was the first time that she had really faced the fact that her mother and Asahel were forever lost to her. She laid her head down on her hands and sobbed out her grief.

The next thing that Miriam knew, the bright light of a torch was flashed into her eyes. She struggled to her feet and heard Anak grunt as some men roughly awakened him with a kick.

"Spies!" a man exclaimed. "I will take them to the officers. The rest of you had best search the area. Where there is one, there may be more."

The sentry led them to a huge field tent and shoved them inside. Within the tent the talk and laughter suddenly ceased, and several of the young men sauntered jauntily to where the new arrivals stood. "What have we here?" one asked.

"Spies!" the sentry replied excitedly. "I caught them loitering along the rim of the Judean camp."

The officer threw back his head in laughter. "And what think you they could hope to spy out there?" he asked when he had regained his breath.

The sentry shrugged sulkily. "It is not mine to know their mission, only to stop it."

Miriam glanced across the room to where several young men were still playing a game. She started as she recognized Urusar among them. She would have called out to him, but Anak closed his hand hard on her arm, silencing her. When she looked up at him, she saw a stern warning in his eyes.

When she looked back, she found that Urusar was watching them, too, but there was nothing in his expression to show that he recognized them. He exchanged a laughing remark with one of his companions and went back to his game. Miriam was suddenly weak with hopelessness. It was, then, just as Yaama had said it would be. She was no longer a cherished friend, but only a bit of the booty of war.

It was possible that Urusar might not have recognized her in her disguise, but he knew Anak quite well. She breathed deeply, tensing herself against the trembling in her knees and in her stomach. Perhaps it was better this way, better to be cruelly tortured, or even killed with a sword, than to be exposed to the indignities of a slave in the households, or the temples, of Babylon.

"If they are spies, why waste time arguing?" a voice demanded.

144

"Aye," another agreed. "Turn them back to the sentry. He can take them outside the camp and dispose of them."

Miriam gasped at the words and found that she was not as ready to die as she had thought. "Take us to Nebuzaradan, captain of the Babylonian forces!" she demanded. "It is he whom we serve."

"Aye, I would not move too hastily," Urusar agreed. He did not even look around as he spoke, but went on with his game. "The old one is in the hire of Nebuzaradan, that much I know. Do I not speak truly, Anak?" he asked.

"Aye, my lord."

Miriam, standing close to her father's old steward, could feel his body tremble, but there was no sign of it in his voice.

"In the name of the gods, Urusar, why stood you there silent?" one of the men demanded.

Urusar shrugged. "Had you asked the old one, he would have told you." He got slowly to his feet and walked to where they stood. "Come," he said brusquely, "I will take you to my uncle's tent."

They walked through the night in silence. At the entrance of Nebuzaradan's tent he stopped and turned angrily to face Miriam. "I had not heard, until this day, that you had returned to the land of Judah! Since then I have set men to searching for you. Did you not know that we would be fearful for your safety?"

"I came as soon as I could."

"Why did you return from the safety of my uncle's house?"

Miriam's eyes filled with tears, and she turned away. "My father was ill," she pleaded. "He was dying and he sent for me. Now he is in his tomb. I knew not where to go, so I came here."

"I am sorry, Miriam," he said gently. "I would do any-

145

thing to make you happy. If you would marry me, I could give you the wealth and honor of my position."

Miriam could scarcely believe what she heard.

"You still find Asahel more pleasing to look upon?" he asked. There was a little of the old teasing in his voice.

Asahel! The thought of him brought a choking lump of misery into her throat. Of all people, he was now most dear to her — and she had offended him. "I would find him exceedingly pleasing to look upon," she said.

Urusar lifted the flap of the tent and led them in. There was only one candle burning in the room. It was at the far side, where a scribe sat writing. Nebuzaradan lay sleeping on a couch nearby, with a slave fanning the air above him.

As her eyes adjusted to the dark interior of the tent, she saw a man whom she had not noticed when she first entered. He sat with his shoulders hunched forward and his face buried in his hands. As she stared in disbelief, he raised his head and their eyes met. In a moment she was kneeling beside him, her eyes searching his face. "Asahel, you are here!"

When he did not answer, she asked, "They captured you and brought you here?"

He shook his head. "Nay. Long have I known that I must come. It was only my own stubborn pride that would not let me admit that I had been wrong."

She let out her breath in a slow sigh of relief. "We waited as long as we dared," she said, smiling up at him, still hardly daring to believe that he had come.

"It was already too late," Asahel explained, "when I reversed my decision, but I felt that I must let our friends know. I spoke with your mother." He paused, looking down at her as though all else, except the wonder of their being

146

together again, was blotted from his mind. Then he smiled, remembering, and added, "She also joined me, for she had long felt in her heart that we went the wrong road. We came on together; she is even now resting in another tent."

Miriam looked up at him, scarcely able to believe what she heard. "My mother?" It was incredible. It was almost more happiness than she could bear. She did not notice that Urusar left the tent, followed by Anak.

After a long silence, Asahel resumed his explanation, "We thought to overtake you, but we must have passed you in the darkness." He put an arm around her and drew her close, laying his cheek against the softness of her hair. "It is all over, my beloved. There will soon be nothing left of Jerusalem, not so much as one stone lying upon another — nothing of Judah. All is lost."

"Nay, Asahel," she whispered. "As long as there is one man and one woman of faith, with Jehovah to lead them, there is hope."

Asahel raised his head slowly and looked down into her upturned face. "I heard what Urusar said to you, Miriam. Would you willingly turn your back upon the luxuries of Babylon, which he offers you, to join me in slavery?" he asked earnestly.

"Wherever you go, I will go."

He took a deep breath and heaved a long, deep sigh, as though suddenly freed of a great weight. "It may never be our good fortune to return to rebuild Jerusalem," he said softly, "but one day Jehovah will return His people to this land."

Miriam nodded her agreement. "And our sons will march with them," she said softly.